BREAK POINT

Michael Shea

This title first published in Great Britain 2001 by
SEVERN HOUSE PUBLISHERS LTD of
9–15 High Street, Sutton, Surrey SM1 1DF.
Originally published 1982 as *Tomorrow's Men*.
This title first published in the USA 2002 by
SEVERN HOUSE PUBLISHERS INC of
595 Madison Avenue, New York, N.Y. 10022.

To Mona, Katriona and Ingeborg

British Library Cataloguing in Publication Data

Shea, Michael,   1938
    Break Point
    1.   Suspense fiction
    I.   Title
    823.9'14 [F]

    ISBN 0-7278-5785-1

Except where actual historical events and characters are being
described for the storyline of this novel, all situations in this
publication are fictitious and any resemblance to living persons
is purely coincidental.

Printed and bound in Great Britain by
MPG Books Ltd., Bodmin, Cornwall.

Preview

Four o'clock on a late September afternoon and a leaden sky hung heavy over the west of the capital. Here and there, despondent clusters of pedestrian activity spawned round the remaining ill-stocked shops and street-markets. A visitor from the recent past would have found a disturbing absence of traffic; for security reasons as much as because of the stringent petrol rationing, few private cars were permitted in central London, while, by the kerb-sides, lay the many vandalised relics of a more prosperous age. What traffic or noise there was was engendered by the police and national security forces, the scout cars of the riot troops, the screaming ambulances and the fire engines whose sirens constantly interrupted the sullen tranquillity. Where it still existed, public transport consisted of elderly, slow-moving Leyland buses, their windows covered in mesh as guard against missiles. Additionally, by night, the food lorries came into the centre of the capital in convoy, guarded doubly against hijacking and common looting.

At a corner of the Old Kent Road, by a church that stood in its abandonment by God and man, the remains of a Jaguar lay askew, as if in some obscene mechanical coupling with the shell of a humble Ford Cortina that was crushed beneath it. Close by, a squad of tattooed and shaven-headed Paramilitaries had caught a young Pakistani woman and were playing with her. She was crying but not struggling too much, since the men were fairly good-natured. Watched and spurred on with cat-calls by their colleagues, three of them were on the point of dragging her in through the broken church door when a black

Mercedes pulled in fiercely alongside the littered pavement. A few yards behind it, a back-up Mercedes, over-filled with heavies, stopped and waited with its engine running. The Commander, a powerful bull of a man with the scars of some not so ancient street battle thrashed in deep scarlet across his forehead, jumped out. Two bodyguards emerged after him. All three men wore the familiar black leather topcoats, each with a Union Jack smartly stitched to the upper right sleeve, the symbol of the United Action Movement.

'Let that Paki go. No fraternisation. You know the rule,' the Commander bellowed. 'No more damned fun and games for you three. For a week, d'you hear? No parades; no night raids; membership-card duties at HQ.'

The three men stood silently to attention as the Commander berated them. The man's voice was powerfully staccato, the words abrasive, but the accent still carried traces of élitist, upper-class vowel sounds. The other Paramils who had automatically lined up in a squad, dressed off to the left in threes, smart in their brushed grey denim uniforms. The Paki girl had taken her chance and disappeared, torn dress clutched around her nakedness. If there were any spectators watching the scene, they were well hidden.

'Who's in charge?'

'I am, Sir,' one of the men, a tight little Cockney, responded.

'Jeffries, isn't it?'

'Yes, Sir.'

The Commander crossed over to him and, in a gesture of basic but effective power, swiped him across the face with the back of his hand. Jeffries flinched but otherwise did not move. 'You're no longer in charge of this squad, Jeffries. I won't have indiscipline. Lucky you're still listed.'

'Sir.'

'We pick precise targets for Number Seven Command. You do only as you're told. I won't have indiscriminate hooliganism. We've a job to do. Concentrate on essentials.' The voice maintained its clipped, unyielding inflection.

'Sir.'

'Your schedule? What is it?'

'Commie picket line at the photo processing lab.'

'Damn you, Jeffries. Get over there. The Riot Unit is outnumbered. At the double. Commandeer a bus if you have to, d'you hear?'

'Sir. At once, Sir.'

The same day; ten minutes to midnight and a different scene. The heavy afternoon sky had broken into a violent drenching thunderstorm which had eventually rolled itself out. The air was clear and fresh, the trees drippingly revived, the ground soft and treacherous underfoot.

The rambling mock-Tudor house stood well back from the edge of Ealing Common. Barbed wire and mesh fencing topped the high garden walls, floodlights illuminated the neatly kept garden and a remarkable array of aerials bedecked the roof. Inside the house itself and to the right of the front door was the cloakroom that served as a guardroom. A large street-map of central London, stubbed with multi-coloured position pins, occupied one entire wall of the little room and on another was a series of party banners proclaiming eternal vigilance against the threat of a Communist take-over. 'If it happened,' one bold-type poster questioned, 'could you look your son in the eye and tell him that you did nothing – nothing to prevent it?' On the third wall, beside the mirror which hung over the cracked washbasin, was sellotaped a large, defiant photograph of the Commander, taken against the background of a triumphant Union Jack.

Two Paramils were on duty in the room, or supposed to be, for one was asleep and the other had taken too many measures from a bottle of looted whisky. From a portable radio came soft mood music. One of the three telephones rang.

'Headquarters Number Seven Command? Recce squad reporting. All quiet. No sign of reprisal groups,' said the voice at the other end. 'Tell the Commander . . .'

3

'That you, Bert? Bert, isn't it?' The guard's words were only slightly slurred. His colleague stirred softly in the battered arm-chair, but slept on.

'Hey – it's you, Geoff? You've got a cushy number tonight . . . Fuckin' good punch up that. We showed those Commie bastards what loyalty means. They won't show their faces at that picket line again.'

'The cops. The frigging comrades are saying the cops were on our side, that they stood by, watched us do it. Just saw their spokesman on the TV . . .'

'Forty of 'em hospitalised. Lucky it wasn't busier at the mortuary. We don't need no cops' help.'

'Maybe it's frigging true though . . .'

'Maybe. They don't like them Commie bastards neither. No way do they.'

There was a pause.

'See you, Bert.'

'See you, Geoff. Hey, how's the Big Boy tonight? Living it up, is he? Any spare birds up there?'

'I don't want no talk like that,' the guard was suddenly aggressive. 'Talk gets around.'

'Sorry, Geoff. Hey, did you get your mitts on some of that Scotch? Fancy that store leaving all that booze on the shelves. Serves 'em right, eh?'

There was a pause.

'Night, Bert.'

'No offence, Geoff?'

'No offence, Bert.'

In a comfortable room upstairs, behind locked and sound-proofed double doors, the Commander was entertaining. The heavy, tightly drawn curtains discreetly hid the steel shutters that were permanently barred over the windows, and the only visible sign of outside tensions was the warning light and alarm buzzer over the doorway.

In his towelling bathrobe, the Commander's guest looked much less impressive than on a television screen or on the floor

4

of the House of Commons. Now he was an intent spectator. Of what it was difficult to see with all the intertwining, but there were four or five girls on the floor in front of him, doing what they were doing in style.

'Discreet, are they?' whispered the Minister nervously sipping at a straight malt and pulling his robe close around an ever-increasing paunch.

'Well paid,' said the Commander. 'And we have additional safeguards . . .'

'I'm sure you have,' said the Minister softly. 'All doubtless tax-deductible.'

'Take your pick. I'll have the rest.' The scar tissue across the Commander's forehead gleamed alternately white and crimson.

Outside, in deep shadows cast by the sodden, vandalised trees of the common, the man whom Fleet Street and the television commentators had nicknamed 'The Brother', to match his opponent, the Commander's title, stood waiting. With him were thirty hand-picked men.

His real name, which few used or even knew, was Paul Verity, Verity the enigma. Borstal boy, Workers' Revolutionary Party, trade union militant, 'the idealist with the burning mission', the leader writers said. Yet they always failed to explain or come to grips with the mission, limited as they were by the terms of traditional political jargon. Paul Verity was too much of an individual to be a Communist, certainly too much of a loner to be a 'brother' to anyone other than in name. But one thing he had was leadership. It was a peculiar charismatic quality in him that quelled argument and inspired loyalty though never affection. What the Commander achieved by violence and his own forms of discipline the Brother obtained by less dramatic but more effective means. The one was a bear with a cudgel, the other had feminine strengths, a vixen, with stiletto claws and eyes that were equally deadly. In more law-abiding times neither man would have ranked higher than a street-gang leader, with only the other and society itself to fight. Now it was different. To each had been given that most dangerous and emotive of all weapons, a cause; for each, that cause was backed by a wider national organisation that invested both of them with even more power and influence, particularly in the London area.

Paul Verity stood still, the hood of a dark anorak framing his thin, hyper-alert face. He and his men waited one hour, then a second. A scout party reported the arrival of the girls and of an unidentified man in a Government Humber. At twelve thirty the men moved, quietly, unhurried, taking their pace from the man who led them. They had prepared their ground well. They knew from their mole which wall, which alarm switch, which wire to cut, which key, which door. In their black face masks and overalls, they looked like nothing more than dancing shadows as they crossed the well-tended lawn. The guard, Geoff, along with his sleeping partner, was pulped with iron bars and bicycle chains. It was a little too noisily done and the Commander and his guest were able to get away by an even better-planned escape route through a cellar at the rear of the house. The five girls had another fate in store for them which in part appeased the Brother's men for the failure of their revenge mission.

Paul Verity himself did not go in for such things.

One

DESPITE the violence of the streets, there were still those who came to the Royal Festival Hall to listen to great music, for on the South Bank life remained cultured and sedate. It was a last expression of the sort of atmosphere which Londoners had created for themselves during the Second World War, even at the height of Hitler's Blitz, the feeling that, Fuehrer or no Fuehrer, culture had to survive, be supported and enjoyed. At another, more popular level, in Soho and the West End, there were still a few theatres and cabarets playing to full houses, despite the fact that the rest of British society seemed intent on bleeding to death from self-inflicted wounds.

From above, unseen, the murmur filtered down as the audience departed from the vast auditorium. As Lou Gregory heard the applause die away, he felt drained in the aftermath of the powerful music. He moved slowly, his leg aching, and he was almost alone in the orchestra pit by the time he had finished rearranging his sheet music and bedding his viola, well wrapped in a soft cloth, into its battered case. As an afterthought, he stopped at the music library and picked up a copy of the following evening's score and slipped it into his briefcase. It had been some time since he had played anything by Grieg; above all, he was conscientious and there would be time to practise at home before the morning's rehearsal.

The dressing room was crowded. He hesitated for a moment in the doorway, eyes behind their pebble glasses half-closed against the strong fluorescent light. One of the horn players, a man who had always kept a gentle eye on his frail yet talented colleague, came up and offered him a drink from a hip flask. 'You need a pick-me-up, Lou,' the man said kindly. 'Best the Balham black market could produce.'

'No . . . No thanks. All I want is a good night's sleep,' Lou heard himself say. Deep down he knew he needed more rest than that.

Then, with some strange, improbable timing, came the voice he knew and a firm unmistakable hand on his shoulder. Lou's eyes lit up and tiredness dropped away. It was for him the ultimate tonic. He turned to come face to face with his other self.

'Max, Max . . . When did you get here? I thought you were . . .'

'The late flight from Oslo.' The familiar voice was of a more self-assertive tone and dimension than was usual in the dressing room. The twin brothers embraced. One or two members of the orchestra looked across, exchanged understanding looks, and went on with their gossip. Lou was popular; they could have no doubts, from the identikit face, who the stranger was. They had heard much about Lou's prosperous brother Max over the years, years of long separation in two lives that had once been so close.

'Good news. Clear ten days before I have to get back to New York. Leisurely Christmas together . . .'

'Christmas? How . . .? Just a moment. Just a moment. Let's . . . let's get out of this damn place.' Lou stuttered with emotion as he began struggling into the ponderous, once elegant coat with its collar of moulting fur. Max came round behind him to calm and help as he had always done. Lou fussed until he found his knitted fawn scarf, wound it unfashionably around his neck, then stuck a dusty black Homburg too low on his head until his ears pressed absurdly outwards. Now he was ready for the icy London night. Only then, still myopically blinking with unconcealed pleasure, did he notice that his brother was lightly clothed in cord jacket, sports shirt and slacks.

'Your overcoat, Max?'

'Just like Mother, Lou. Always were. Don't fuss. It's warm after Oslo. Tropical compared with the Forties rig I was on this morning.'

'A coat. Ah, wait. . . I have that old brown one in my locker. I was going to get the nightwatch to give it away.'

'I bet you were. I remember it from student days.'

Lou bustled off to reappear moments later with a rough tweed coat. Max reluctantly took it. 'Like as two peas,' the horn player said to a colleague as Lou waved goodnight and the two men left the dressing room.

Likeness there was up to a point in intellect and features but the brothers were far from similar in life style, interests and physique. Lou thought, talked, lived for his music. He was not a great soloist but had played with moderate success in many of the world's orchestras, and was known and liked within his limited circle. Under the fur-lined coat, the stiff white shirt and the evening dress, the body was oily white, too tired and wasted for his fifty-five years. Max, by contrast, whilst he liked listening to music, particularly when his brother was playing, had been built for power. Robust and tanned, he was the perpetual bread-winner who had paid for his brother's last years at the Royal Academy of Music after their school-teacher father had died. Abrasive and ambitious, Max was well fitted for his role as head of the Gregory Institute, one of the most competitive think-tanks in the whole United States. He was the international super-consultant of whom it was said that he was listened to by more premiers, sheiks and presidents than any man not in high government office.

'Bus or walk, Max?'

'Lou, you look dead beat. Let's pick up a cab. How's your leg?'

'No, no. Not for me. Any case . . . taxis are like gold dust these days. The leg's fine. Not nearly so stiff now . . . after the operation. The night air . . . seeing you again . . . A walk is what I need. Keep exercising it, the doctor says.'

From the Festival Hall there is a pedestrian way along that

part of the Thames Embankment which is paved with great grey concrete slabs. In the past it was always thronged after a concert; now it was deserted. Across the icy river, Big Ben and the Houses of Parliament shone their lights inadequately through a first flurry of snow that was dusting a sheen of purity over the litterstrewn stones. Somewhere downstream, the ever-haunting sound of a ship's siren echoed. Below, on the river itself, a police launch patrolled the polluted waters, its engine thudding rhythmically against the tide. It was a London night through which Alfred Hitchcock might have stalked.

By Westminster Bridge, deserted except for a solitary double decker bus with its mesh-covered windows, the two brothers turned down below the high perimeter fence that encircled St Thomas' Hospital. As they passed, from the far end of the bridge, a blaze of searing light swept its inquisitive beam to and fro across the roadway. A fierce shadow was suddenly cast by one of the jaded stone lions that guard the Headquarters of the Greater London Council. The searchlight came from one of the check points which the Grenadier Guards, who had long abandoned their bearskins and scarlet tunics for more levelling khaki, now manned at the entrances to the safe area around Whitehall and the tarnished Mother of Parliaments. The southern Embankment of the Thames was well lit at that point; the Victorian cast-iron lamps, fashioned in the shape of huge dolphins, had unsightly but effective arc lights strung in a row between them. Everywhere the obnoxious litter of the run-down city lay as evidence of the continuing strike by the majority of its public service employees.

'I never walk on my own these days,' Lou was saying. 'One of the last joys of London is out for me now. I travel by bus everywhere. It's safer.'

'Which pack would I side with if I lived here?' responded Max Gregory. 'Hell if I know, Lou. I'm glad I'm through having to choose any more. It's bad enough in the States.'

'You vote?' Lou was aware of his brother's political cynicism.

'In the event, no. But there's usually a smattering of justification for favouring one lot over the other.'

A hundred yards in front, a bend in the wall created a shallow pocket of shadow that seemed all the more intense because of the brightness of the arc lights around. It was sufficient to hide two figures who stood in silence, blending with the night, waiting for the brothers as they approached.

'My suitcase; I saw it come out of the baggage chute. Then, when I went to get it, it had gone. Someone had lifted it . . . I had to fill in a claim form, which is why I missed the concert.'

'Airline incompetence. It'll turn up. Was there much . . .?'

'Clothes, my coat, a few papers and . . . a present for you.'

'For me?' Lou Gregory looked across, an expression of childish gratification on the prematurely ageing face.

'Don't worry. I can replace it.'

'What . . .?'

'Tut, tut, Lou. Wait till Christmas morning.'

Lou began to laugh, but it was a sound that died in his throat.

'What's . . .' He grabbed his brother's arm as the two figures moved out of the shadows.

'Relax. They look like ordinary policemen to me.' The brothers walked quickly on, making to pass the officers.

'Evening,' Max said agreeably.

'Not so fast.' One of the policemen moved to block their way. Max noted that both had their gun holsters unfastened.

'Papers. I'll look in that violin case too . . . and the briefcase.'

'What's the matter . . .?' Max began.

'Leave it, Max,' Lou said. 'It's normal. These bombs. There have been two or three today already.'

'Five,' said the policeman bleakly. He thumbed through Lou's identity book, then took hold of Max's US passport. It was an offence, punishable by up to three months in prison, to travel without papers. Two years ago, when identity books were first issued to every adult, it had been different. The other officer rummaged through the sheet music in Lou's briefcase, then turned to search the viola case. His methods were far from gentle and the instrument nearly fell out onto the ground. Aghast at damage being done to such a valued possession, Lou jerked forward to catch it.

The policeman reacted urgently, hand dropping automatically to hover by his open holster. 'Keep your distance, you. I won't harm the bloody thing.'

'Right,' barked the other officer. 'Up against the wall – both of you. Move.'

The brothers did as they were bid, standing feet apart, hands outspread. They waited. They waited for five minutes that seemed like hours, hands freezing against the harsh stone. Max turned his head slightly to try to look at the policemen. One of them had a gun, the other was muttering into his two-way radio.

'Can't you search us and let us go? My brother's not well . . .' Max began.

'Face the bloody wall. Move again and we'll take you in,' came the response.

'Gently, Max,' whispered Lou. 'Gently.'

Ten minutes passed. The policemen still made no move to search them. It had begun to snow quite heavily, and Max, for the first time, appreciated his brother's coat. Then came a bleep from the police radio followed by the crackle of a message that was totally inaudible to the brothers.

'OK. You can go now. But make direct to Vauxhall. No turning off. Both sides have gangs out in force. You've been warned.'

'Thank you, Officer,' said Lou softly.

The brothers moved on along the Embankment, their feet indenting the fresh snow. 'That copper was nervous as hell when you . . . He thought you were going to attack him,' Max said.

'Can't blame him. A hundred police killed this year in London alone.'

'Can I talk about that, Lou? Why not come back with me? With your contacts you'd get a job in New York, easy. Until you do – my apartment . . . you like New York and I'm not often there. You'd have it to yourself.'

'My contract with the orchestra has six months to run. Not going to sponge on you. Not any more I'm not.'

'Come off it, Lou. I miss seeing you. We . . . we do so well together. While the troubles . . . till the London scene cools a bit. Worried to hell about you living where you do.' For a moment Max Gregory betrayed feelings that he had long trained himself to hide.

'I'm all right. Need to be careful, that's all.'

'But see . . . Oh, never mind. Hey, let me take that viola for a bit. You've got enough with your briefcase.'

'I can manage.'

'Give me.' Max took the viola case, taking the decision as he always had done for the only person who mattered in his rigorous life.

Behind them, back along the Embankment, one of the policemen was standing with a civilian who was dressed in the standard garb of the plainclothes men from Section Nine: brown felt hat and grey military-styled mackintosh. The other policeman had disappeared.

'Brothers – twins. Identical birthdates. One's a musician. He's carrying a fiddle in a case,' reported the policeman.

'What else?' asked the man in the felt hat.

'The musician's wearing a brown coat. The other, with the US passport, is dressed in a heavy coat with a fur collar and a black hat.'

'Right. Report back to Section Nine. Now.' The civilian turned and walked away.

'Hell . . . was it the other way around?' the policeman thought as he watched the departing figure merge into the thickening snow. He shrugged. It would work out the same in the end.

The brothers had reached the network of streets by Vauxhall Bridge. All around there the buildings were arson-gutted, reeking of social decay.

'We must take a bus from here. It's safer,' said Lou. 'That policeman was . . .'

'Have you food?'

'Not much.'

'I'll get some eggs and bacon. There's a corner shop that still appears to be open over there.'

'You'll be lucky,' said Lou. 'They'll be out of anything fresh.'

'We'll see what enough money will buy,' said Max. 'I won't be a minute.' He walked rapidly across to the shop, still clutching the viola case. Lou watched him, suddenly feeling very much alone. Perhaps New York wasn't such a bad idea. He was no hero. He would tell Max that he had changed his mind. The orchestra's contract had a break clause. He limped over to follow Max into the shop.

Suddenly there were five of them, young men, none older than twenty. Close cropped or shaven heads, identical grey jumpsuits, they stood silent in a precise line between Lou and the barricaded shop-front. He moved forward. They would stand aside. He was defenceless; an elderly lame musician. They pushed him over easily, then went into him with steel-capped boots. There was surprisingly little noise after the first blow but they kept at it, burying the shattered spectacle glass into the face and eyes, going for the throat, stomach and groin.

Inside the ill-stocked shop, the unshaven shopkeeper turned down the sound on the television set to hear what the man in the brown tweed coat wanted. His other hand rested discreetly on the little shelf below the counter where, beside the button that controlled the automatic lock on the door, a handgun lay at the ready with its safety catch off. As the noise of the television died leaving a flickering black and white Western epic rolling soundless across the screen, the two men became aware of the scuffle outside.

'The gangs again. I'll bolt the door shutters,' said the shopkeeper picking up his gun with a sudden burst of speed and coming out from behind the counter. 'You can wait here till they've gone. With luck they'll leave me alone but they don't like no strangers.'

14

'Lou. . .' Max Gregory turned with something approaching a roar, and beat the man to the door handle. Outside, the youths were kicking at a dark misshapen bundle lying on the fresh clean snow. Gregory turned again and, with an agility born of desperation, seized the gun from the startled shopkeeper's hand. He was still absurdly clutching his brother's viola case in the other hand as he ejected himself back into the street. With a torrent of base invective the shopkeeper slammed the door behind him, bolted the shutters, and extinguished all the lights.

Outside, two of the young men turned to face Max. 'Fuck off, fiddler. We don't want you,' one said.

The two youths, now joined by the other three, advanced on Max Gregory in a viciously contracting semi-circle. They were laughing, for they had not seen the gun. Suddenly one darted forward and with a well-aimed kick from his steel-capped boot knocked the viola case hurtling from Gregory's grasp. The box struck the snow-covered ground and burst open. The youth bent forward, peered contemptuously at the viola, then brought his foot down, crushing the instrument into an ugly mess of gut and sheer edges of lovingly polished wood.

'The hero come to rescue 'is fuckin' brother, 'as he?' The leader of the pack spat his words in mockery. 'Well, well. Too late, man. Too fuckin' late. They said Maxie boy there would be tough. You're the weak one, they said. So you should be really easy. Are you easy, Lou?' The leader laughed and turned to seek appreciation from his colleagues who cat-called back in unison: 'Easy. . . Easy.'

'Well, in that case, fiddler . . . Goodbye.'

The youths paced around him slowly, like jackals sizing up their prey, waiting for him to freeze in some primitive fear. Behind them the street was totally deserted though there were those who, with the shopkeeper, watched the developing scene through unwashed windows and through gaps in faded curtains.

Gregory moved first and fast, spinning out an arc of death, pulling the trigger again and again. The youths, caught by surprise by the noise and the spattered fire, turned and ran – or three of them did, for the other two lay dead or dying at his feet. Stepping over a prostrate body which was already painting the snow dark red beneath it, Gregory bent over, lifted his brother's broken body and carried it across to the shop door. He did not need to look closely to know that he carried a corpse. There he gently laid his brother out across the broad top step with the old brown coat folded as a useless pillow under his head. Then he straightened up, knocked, then hammered and shook the bars. And because the shopkeeper would not open up, he shot through the locking bolt, pulled aside a shutter, broke the door and climbed in. He found the light, then the terrified shopkeeper hiding in a back room, then a telephone. Before he left, he stopped briefly by the body at the door, his head bowed, his eyes dry.

Eventually a police squad and an ambulance came screaming through the snow to take Lou and the two youths to the mortuary. Of Max Gregory there was no sign. As a matter of routine, the police pulled the shopkeeper in for questioning. They wouldn't even let him lock up his shop first, but then they were busy that night as every night and no one actually got round to interrogating him. He was released in the bitter, early hours of the next day and went back to start, weary but resigned, clearing up the pitiful remnants of his looted shop.

The mood of the times was such that the incident did not even warrant a report in the press.

The condition of the times was also such that official screening of passengers departing from Heathrow for Paris the following morning was arbitrary and lax. Nonetheless, the CIA's Head of London Station accompanied by the Head of the London Bureau of the Gregory Institute, a partially reformed alcoholic called Mason, personally saw Professor Max Gregory to the plane and reconfirmed his Air France Concorde booking from Charles de Gaulle Airport on to New York, Kennedy. It was a further measure of Gregory's importance that the Station Head had himself delivered a message from the White House which finally persuaded Gregory that nothing was to be gained by his remaining in London to face a multiple homicide charge. Through inter-mediaries, the CIA would ensure a proper burial for his brother Lou.

In the departure lounge, Mason emerged with the mislaid suitcase. Perhaps the papers it contained had been tampered with, but to the inexpert eye, even the top coat, even the gift-wrapped antique brass and walnut metronome, were intact. Which accounted for everything except that a gang of hoods had been set to kill a man and had killed his brother instead.

Two

NEW YORK: one month later to the day. Below its green glass shade the desk lamp spilled a pool of light across the neat piles of computer print-outs, agency reports and teleprinter tear-sheets on the polished mahogany surface. From the window came a brasher reflection from a huge neon sign high on a building on the other side of Madison Avenue. The only other illumination in the office emanated from the flickering blue and white television screen where Reuter's News Service flashed its abbreviated summary of the day's catalogue of tragedies.

Framed by a wall of overladen bookshelves, Max Gregory sat, slouched low in a leather easy chair. All around him were signs of comfortable taste: it was more an academic's study than the functional nerve-centre of the Gregory Institute. A report, bound in a neat black folder with the one emotive word *Secret* red-stamped diagonally across it, lay neglected in his lap as he watched the late item of news appearing, line by line, in front of him:

London, Wednesday, January 19: Prime Minister Hunt summoned the British Cabinet into emergency session today amid the chaos of a general strike, galloping inflation and further rumours of an attempted left-wing coup.

There was a pause, the screen cleared, then came the follow-up:

Leftist bombers struck at several Government targets in central London. At least forty people reported killed or injured. Massive right-wing counter-demonstrations in the streets of several major British cities.

Again, after a gap, the screen refilled:

State Department is following events closely. Remaining American subjects in Britain are being advised by US Embassy to stay off the streets.

The British story was replaced by one about a gigantic earthquake in China. Many thousands were reported dead.

Gregory pulled himself out of his chair with more appearance of effort than his fifty-five years justified and crossed his office to turn off the set. Distant tragedies lost their proportion and China was a far-away land of which he knew little. To him, even after fifteen years of self-imposed exile, Britain was still Britain, even if it was enmeshed in an apparently inevitable process of self-destruction. Unread in his hand he held the secret file which had come, like so many of the other reports lying on his desk, from the CIA, who were the generous backers of the most important of the Gregory Institute's current research projects. They provided money and raw information, and Gregory, accepting it as part of the great American way of government, fed back reports and analyses to CIA Headquarters at Langley, Virginia. For public consumption his project was on UK oil reserves, but a secret protocol signed by Gregory and by Admiral Cassover, the Director of the CIA, laid down a wider and more significant brief for the Institute. It was, in a nutshell, a covert operation to monitor and assess all political and economic developments in the UK for the CIA. For they were back in the big intelligence league again after the long, lean, over-exposed Nixon-Ford-Carter years, and who better to master-mind such a project for them than Professor Gregory, a man of British extraction who could come and go at will, who could meet people at every level in British political life without being an identifiable agent of the US Administration? Gregory refused to feel himself a traitor to his background by holding this extra brief; he was, after all, a mere searcher after truth, or that at least was his justification to the only person to whom he was answerable on this score: himself.

Gregory moved from the television set across the deep carpeting to the picture window and stared down the forty prosperous storeys to where the evening traffic laboured its way up Madison Avenue. While Britain was on the brink, New York, away below, with all its problems, was still very much alive and well. But for him, for the thousandth time in only a month, the two, the present and the past, were intermeshed, dominated by the memory of a shapeless human bundle on snow-flecked cobblestones. At that moment he was only remotely aware of the present: raucous sirens of the NYPD and the bull-horns that backed up the flashing lights of a fire engine as it forced a path between reluctant automobiles two blocks away. Gradually the noise grew fainter, leaving behind the distant sound of tyres on wet asphalt and the horns of jamstuck drivers impatient to gain their destinations.

It was eight in the evening and most of the Gregory Institute staff had left for the day. One or two of those closest to Gregory had looked in on their way home to exchange last minute views on the current state of Britain. They were the same colleagues who, knowingly or unknowingly, had contributed to the current CIA Personality Assessment on Gregory that had been produced for Admiral Cassover before the secret protocol had been promulgated. The overwhelming view of all those who worked with him was that, though it would never be allowed to affect his judgement and there was little evidence to support it, even he must surely be upset by what was happening over there. Yet he was an utterly private man, the assessment read, a loner who never allowed his defences to slip. Even when he had returned from London a month ago, several days had had to elapse before his colleagues discovered, via CIA Liaison themselves, that he had so recently witnessed his brother's assassination in a London street. Such ice-cold lack of emotion simply reinforced the views of Gregory's colleagues. They had long appreciated the need to match the impersonal correctness of his relations with them, that feelings were strictly out of court at the Institute, that employees were expected to be hard-nosed, dispassionate analysts of world crises, followers of the rule that to get personally involved in a problem was bad *per se* and only led to emotion-biased judgements. Gregory had never sought their sympathies just as he rejected any intrusion by them into his private beliefs.

Turning to examine his professional and private life style, the CIA Assessment noted that during the office day he was demanding, brilliant, abrasive, offering in return all the qualities of leadership that, in fifteen years in an alien city, had brought him to the top of one of the hardest professions of all – the sale of intellect. They had been years through which he had pulled himself up from near poverty and had, equally ruthlessly, dragged with him the old-fashioned firm of business consultants he had bought. That firm was now far from old-fashioned, and, with its name changed to the Gregory Institute for International Affairs, it was among the best financed and respected think-tanks in the field, competing vigorously with the Rand Corporation and the Hudson Institute in selling talent and acting as super-consultants to the highest bidder. All this in a country and a city where success is the pre-eminent value.

Gregory's co-workers were unable to volunteer to the CIA much information about him outside the office and away from the policy lunches and weekend seminars that were the only semi-social extensions of his office discipline. At various times some of them reported that they had tried to get through to him by inviting him to their Long Island villas, or for weekends at their New England academic retreats. Only old man Riverton, the former president of the business consultancy Gregory had taken over, had his invitation accepted. Riverton had refused to cooperate or confirm the story that the weekend had not been an entire success and that thereafter he had kept relations with his protégé strictly within the office walls. If Riverton had been saddened, as others said, by failing to reach an understanding with his junior, he kept this to himself but he did make it clear that he knew the worth when he saw it of the younger man's abilities as a manager and his genius as a public affairs analyst. Who was more accomplished than Gregory at spotting the value of a proposal or developing a concept before anyone else had focused on it? The CIA Personality Assessment noted that the only occasion when long-term colleagues remembered a display of anything approaching warmth had been some years previously when Max Gregory's twin brother had come from London to visit him and he had been shown round the Institute. Then there had been smiles and glasses of sherry and brief humanity and a glimpse of the bachelor who felt for someone other than himself.

Again, some years ago and in less permissive times, the assessment noted, lurid stories had gained currency of Gregory having been seen in unconventional surroundings with even more unconventional escorts. For a brief season, his name appeared in the gossip columns of the *Post* and *News*, with him branded as constant companion to one of the more notorious actresses appearing at that time off Broadway. The facts were many-sided: the actress had pursued him and had publicised their almost non-existent affair to satisfy her agent's bid to add intellectual glamour to her reputation. Gregory's life, by contrast, had been a mixture of all-consuming work at the Institute, punctuated by rare, short-lived affairs that were kept entirely private.

Gregory pulled himself away from the window and went to sit behind his desk where he began to study the secret CIA file he had been holding. The first two documents in it were standard daily intelligence reports from UK regional stations.

Report CZ 91/11/84: Belfast, Ulster: Wednesday, January 19: Political leaders in Northern Ireland are monitoring the situation in mainland Britain with ever-increasing concern. The Reverend Sean MacArthur, Leader of the Centre Unity

Party, has issued a statement urging his political colleagues in Westminster to show every restraint in reacting to the current situation. 'I speak from bitter experience,' stated the Reverend MacArthur, 'when I say that nothing is to be achieved by giving support either in verbal or in practical terms to the street-corner leaders and gangs who believe that violence is the only means of achieving their political ends.'

Worried by events on the mainland disturbing the relatively peaceful situation currently prevailing in Ulster, the Commander-in-Chief of the UN Supervisory Force in Northern Ireland, Colonel Ahmed El-Araf, echoed this view when he addressed an inter-denominational rally in South Armagh today. The rally was also attended by the leader of the All-Ireland Protestant Movement and Dublin's Minister for Ecumenical Affairs, Mrs Isobel Levy.

Report CZ 92/8/84: Glasgow, Scotland: Wednesday, January 19: A number of houses in the prosperous West End of the City were destroyed by fire last night in one of the worst outbreaks of sectional violence in recent weeks. There were three so-called commando raids into fashionable Bearsden again yesterday, leading to widespread arson and looting. A number of deaths have been reported, but given the breakdown of effective communications between police and the residual emergency services in the west of Scotland, precise figures of those killed and injured are impossible to obtain. Appeals by Church leaders for calm have so far failed to have any noticeable effect. Clydeside and the greater Glasgow conurbation is now in the twelfth day of an all-out general strike. Electricity and water supplies are continually being interrupted, and it is reported that food supplies are failing to reach many central areas of the city. By contrast, the black market is flourishing . . .

The third input in the secret file was an even more delicate excerpt, dated eleven days previously, from British Cabinet Committee Minutes on UK oil resources. It would, Gregory wondered, be interesting to know how the CIA had acquired it, whom they had bought it from and for how much. But for the present it was content that mattered. The first page of the minutes listed the composition of the committee, something he knew was crucial information when one was assessing the value to be put on any report on any subject, anywhere.

Energy Resources Sub-Committee; Tuesday, January 8; Eleventh Session; Fifth Meeting: Chairman: Prime Minister. Present: Secretary of State for Energy, Chancellor of the Exchequer, Secretary of State for Scotland, Minister for Industry, Minister without Portfolio. Secretary of Sub-Committee: Miss Eileen Byrne, Cabinet Office, Whitehall, London, SW1.

He paused in his reading, closed his eyes and rested his head against the leather back of his chair. That name . . . He remembered the British girl with the auburn hair because she had stood out from all the others: ten, eleven years ago, and she had been a post-graduate student at Columbia, researching a thesis on energy policy and paying her own way through college by working as an Assistant Economist at the Gregory Institute. Of medium height, when she stood close to him as she eventually did, she had reached to just above the level of his shoulder . . . Her?

Gregory had been alone in his study. In his outer office, beyond a discreet door plate which read 'Office of the Vice-President', Eileen Byrne had stayed late to try to catch up with her employer's highly demanding workload. At short notice she had moved in to take the place of his elderly permanent assistant when the latter had to go into hospital with an infection of an unused area of her inner anatomy. Eileen told him later how fortunate she thought herself to have the chance to work for such a well-known man, and that, from the outset, she had been intent on showing what a good permanent replacement she would make. Much later she admitted to

24

social objectives as well, since the icy arrogance of her employer had, over the few weeks that she had been at the Institute, produced a reverse effect on her. A severe hairstyle and overlarge intellectual spectacles, the blue-stocking symbols of those years, were carefully deployed so as not entirely to disguise her potentially attractive body.

When she entered the room that particular evening, Gregory had been staring out of the window, and if he was aware of her, he made no move until she began to rearrange an already well-ordered desk top. A methodical man, he was about to turn round and express irritation, but she had spoken first.

'Everything OK, Professor? Is there anything else?'

'No, thank you. Good night, Eileen.' He did not face her and his voice was dismissive.

'I think . . . I'm managing to get the hang of things. Quite some pressure . . .' She had been a little thrown by continuing to address Gregory's back.

'Yes, fine. Just fine.' With reluctance he had turned round, his head bent at the angle at which he had been staring down into the avenue far below. Thus he found himself focusing less on her face than on her body where he saw, readily enough, that one too many buttons on her white shirt-front was undone.

'Good night,' he repeated.

She stood her ground. 'I'm enjoying it,' she said, a fraction lamely, unwilling to give up without a struggle. She told him later that she had seen the direction of his eyes and had stared back at him, willing his coldness to evaporate. He had looked hard at her then, realising how young she was, that she was only looking for some personal contact. But he saw too that she had ambition and intellect, both of which were great aphrodisiacs in Gregory's attitude to women. She would probably be an avid reader of women's cult literature on such things; now she would also have to face old-fashioned masculine indications of lust.

'Good night,' she had said, turning towards the door.

He had smiled. 'You've been working hard. Sit down. Tell me about yourself. Where d'you come from in Britain?' He paused. 'A drink? I'm about to have one. Scotch OK?' He had not waited for any of her replies but began pouring out whisky from a decanter at a corner cocktail cabinet.

'I . . . yes . . . London . . . Thank you,' she said, taking the proffered glass. She had remained standing.

'Enjoying New York, are you? How long have you been here . . .?' His questions were not ones which required or were given time for answers. He continued to stare at her as she raised a hand to do up a recently undone button.

'I wouldn't bother. We're both adult, are we not?' Before she had time to grasp what he was saying, he'd moved on again. 'Let me guess: twenty-three?'

The hand fluttered back to her side. 'Nearly . . . next month.' With her other hand she had held her glass and sipped compulsively.

'And tonight you stayed . . .' He noticed for the first time, even in the dull light, how green her eyes were and the soft sheen of her auburn hair.

'I . . . er . . .' she began.

'We are both adult . . . British . . .' he repeated, then suddenly had chosen to become arrogantly direct. 'So . . . we both know why you stayed.'

'I don't . . . I wouldn't jump to conclusions.' She took a further gulp from her glass.

'If one doesn't jump at them they change.' He moved a little way towards her and she drew back.

'I think I . . .'

'Oh I don't think so. You don't want to do that. Not now; not after all that effort.'

'What do you mean?'

He came up quite close to her and waited in silence for some moments as if sizing her up. She had not moved, as if aware of the inevitable.

'Yes or no?' he asked, then without waiting, brought his hand up suddenly behind her neck, pulling her forward, almost savagely. He kissed her, she began to struggle, then went limp as he dominated her. Equally suddenly he let her go and she almost fell. He stood back after that, watching her, then turned and went over to his leather arm chair and sat down. Leaning back, legs slightly apart and stretched out lazily in front of him, he looked across at her.

'Lock the door.'

'I must . . .'

'Do you want to stay or don't you? The Ops Room boys are still here. When they know I'm working late, they often burst in with the latest tapes.' The matter-of-fact statement threw her even more. She turned and did as bidden.

'Now the blinds.' He continued to watch impassively as she pulled the cords to close the slats. By now he could have told her to do anything and she would have done it. He told her what he wanted.

'Please . . . please . . . not like this.'

'You may go if you wish.'

She hesitated, then began, first blouse, then her smock, then the rest. She stood to face him.

'You're quite . . . you have a fierce style.'

'Style?' At last he laughed, almost kindly. 'And you like it . . . you have a good body. Now take your spectacles off; unloose your hair . . . There, that's better. Why do academic women feel the need to hide it all?'

'Please . . . not like this,' Eileen repeated, coming hesitantly towards him. She shivered, showing how young she still was.

'Yes, like this. Stay where you are. *I* like it. *You* like it. That's what matters. Now turn . . . more . . . And round . . . now, down . . .'

'Oh, I can't . . .'

'Now over to me . . . See . . . you do it well. Over here . . . right over . . .'

She was crying as she left and did not return his 'Good night, Eileen.' By the end he had softened a great deal and had kissed her gently. He told himself that it was more as an insurance policy to gain her silence than from any real feeling. If she came back . . . he would have to speak to Personnel

Section and have them find him a new temporary assistant . . . ugly and old.

But even in the cold light of the next day he did not do so and she had stayed working for him until she gained the mastery of him. Three months after that she left.

Eleven years on, Gregory poured himself a whisky and settled at his desk to read the forgotten British Cabinet Committee Minutes. Below the list of committee members came the single sentence conclusion.

The Committee agreed that, provided foreign development finance continues to be forthcoming, is not discouraged by or can continue to be insured against current UK domestic disorders, the overall prospects for future North Sea oil production, particularly in the Unst fields, remain good. *Signed*: Eileen Byrne, Secretary of Sub-Committee.

Three

TWO HOURS later he was still at his desk when the intercom light flashed.

'Yes? . . . Yes. You have him on the line now? . . . Tell him I'm coming.'

Gregory thrust his way out of his office, along the dimly lit corridor and through the swing doors into the neon brightness of the Ops Room. A young clerk at a computer console glanced up, then went back to his programming. He had been warned not to cross eyes with the boss.

'You're tired, Mason.' Gregory eased himself into the high steel chair opposite the Institute's newly installed videophone.

'Damn these machines. We'll need make-up before dialling a call in future . . . Yes, hell knows I'm tired. Twenty-one-hour day, third day running. Three a.m. and no way finished, Max.' Mason, as head of the Institute's London Bureau, was one of the few who first-named with Professor Gregory.

Gregory moved his eyes from the screen to take in the battery of digital clocks that showed world time, then swung back to watch Mason's pockmarked, unshaven face.

'What's sterling going to do when London opens?'

'Only one thing . . . down . . . if it opens, that is. Word is that the Chancellor may keep the Bank and the exchanges closed tomorrow . . . today.'

'With your salary in dollars . . .'

'It's the only thing that keeps me here. You know that, Max.'

'So what else is new?'

'Cabinet meeting broke up half an hour ago.'

'And?'

'They don't matter any more.'

'What happened?'

'It got worse, that's all. They came out talking to the press and to anyone else who would listen, trying to prove how right they are.'

'What about?'

'Street gangs wildly out of control – there was a mini-war again tonight; accusations of the police siding with the United Action Movement; rumours of ministers in secret negotiation with extremists; the BBC being attacked by both sides for lack of impartiality. They're on a hiding to nothing with all these problems. Then there's the army. With them it's only a short step from assisting the Civil Power in strike-breaking and combating political terrorism, to the generals wanting much more power when the troops do get called in.'

'Military coup?'

'One current option.'

'And behind it?'

'Why should anyone be? Anarchy. Plain anarchy.'

'What's Hunt's solution? He's no political eunuch. Didn't he . . .'

'Eunuch . . .? You don't know what happened to Hunt tonight?' Mason's eroded face stared back questioningly from the screen. 'Of course not. It would miss your evening news bulletins. So . . . watch while I play a chunk of video news film.'

Mason's face cleared itself from the set. After a few moments a picture came on line: a civic banquet in some still prosperous outskirt of London. Ladies in sensible hats were in the majority at the elegant tables, though there were a number of local dignitaries including a mayor who was sporting a chain of office across his ample chest. Then, heralding the guest of honour's arrival, nervous officials and a phalanx of implacable security men entered the dining room. The well-modulated voice of the BBC commentator described the scene as, to a burst of cheering, Harold Hunt, the pudgy, horn-rimmed British Prime Minister, moved to take his place at the rostrum. To Gregory, sitting thousands of miles away in New York, Hunt's whole manner, the heavy smiles acknowledging the applause, reeked of self-complacency as it had always done even before the man's most recent return to power. Like a bad actor, this particular would-be world statesman had come out of retirement, like a poor man's de Gaulle, to save a nation that was almost beyond salvation.

Gregory noted that the Prime Minister spoke without notes; his phrases were so over-used, he would know them by heart. 'I am most grateful, Madam Chairman, Mr Mayor, for inviting me here today. I am sorry I could not make your meal, but looking on the bright side, coming in at the end of it as it were, at least my speech won't give you all indigestion.' The laughter followed obediently on cue, the PM paused, then turned heavily serious: 'There are, Madam Chairman, those who would divide our people. There are those who think they can lead by ever more violent means, that politics is made on the street corners. The press and television, interested only in the sensational, give too much coverage, too much status to street gangs and their leaders . . .'

Gregory had already had enough of Hunt's nasal north-country platitudes when it happened. The BBC cameraman, with prize-winning dedication, caught every detail of what followed. His lens was combing the increasingly somnolent faces of the well-dined suburban audience as they reacted to the Prime Minister's words which flowed as a dirge of background sound. Suddenly a young man was standing amongst the hats and the white and silver of the tables. He shouted meaningless, inaudible slogans, until he drowned his own words with the rattle of fire from the sub-machine gun which he swung from his hip. The cameraman held his ground and the lens recorded everything, the screams, the panic as people threw themselves to the floor, the gun jamming, the crowd moving in and jumping on the youth, well-polished shoes kicking, Gucci handbags flailing. Then, too late, the camera watched as the security men, handguns at the alert, moved into action. With the continuing screams as background sound, the film moved to show, coldly and without surprise or compassion, death horridly set out along the high table – blood and red roses intermingled.

The screen cleared and Mason's face reappeared. He spoke without emotion. 'Hunt was found huddled below the lectern, unhurt, totally and absolutely unhurt. Seven others killed and about the same number wounded.'

'Left or right wing?'

'Does it matter? Another "anti". Probably Marxist-Anarchist. Badly torn and beaten by the crowd. Point is, Hunt was in no mood to chair any Cabinet meeting. Even the law-and-order gang couldn't get him on their side. He just sat there mumbling to himself.'

'I get the mood. Useful for tomorrow.'

'What's tomorrow?'

'Washington: White House. Cassover wants me to go down and support him, I guess. Auerbach and he are in the midst of another spat about what to do about Britain, and I'm to be fall guy in front of the President.'

There was a pause, then Mason decided to risk his other piece of news. 'They got nowhere in tracing the origins of the louts you killed.'

The response was as cold as they come. 'Tell me when I see you. I'm coming over on Tuesday. Book me in somewhere close.'

'Not very clever if you do. The police want to talk to you. They were angry when you skipped.'

'I'll be a judge of that. Tuesday, OK?'

'Whoopee,' said Mason. It did not look as if he was even trying to smile.

As Gregory was driven home to his East 57th Street apartment later that night, his mind was still at work revising the final chapter of his best-known book, *Britain at the Brink*. The publication of the book had earned him both a great deal of public praise and also the CIA contract in the United States, but it had attracted an equally virulent amount of criticism in Britain itself. 'Cheap and unbalanced polemic by a turncoat British would-be political analyst,' *The Times* had called it in one of the kinder pieces of criticism levelled against it. 'Who is this man Gregory, with his vicious and ill-considered manifesto for despair?' screamed an *Express* leader. By contrast, Gregory himself still believed it to be a moderate analysis of irrefutable past events which had inevitably led to the present state of near anarchy. All he felt he had done was to describe what had happened and then add a foretaste of things to come. The early chapters had taken Britain from the 'toothless bulldog lacking a role' phase, through the decade and a half of the Northern Ireland crises, ever increasing inflation and the mounting millions of unemployed. Then had come the race riots and the anarchy of the streets that the authorities had for some time managed to contain and isolate in areas of metropolitan decay.

The introduction, [Gregory had written] of proportional representation into the voting system was only one of the factors that did indeed, as its critics had warned, bring about a fragmentation of the traditional Westminster party structure. In terms of active politics there are consequently now only three major groupings that matter in Britain today, each of them, in itself, a constantly changing coalition of a number of small parties or political movements. The centralist Government under Premier Hunt, the Central Democratic Alliance (CDA), is largely composed of former Liberals, Social Democrats, right-wing Labourites and left-of-centre Tories. While there still are Conservative and Labour parties in existence, each with numbers of MPs nominally at Westminster (the House of Commons was suspended indefinitely after the riots in the Chamber early last year), the two other real groupings are those on the extreme right and left of the political spectrum, both of which have their power base in the streets, rather than through any democratic process. Of these, the first, the Commander's United Action

33

Movement (UAM), has, as its main policy objectives, a massive build-up of Britain's defence capabilities, a tough law and order programme including internment and forced labour camps for 'socially undesirable elements', repatriation of all West Indian and Asian minorites, the outlawing of the Communist Party, and stringent government controls over national resources such as North Sea oil and gas, to avoid these assets falling into the hands of non-British companies and individuals.

By contrast, the left-wing coalition, the People's Socialist Coalition (PSC), under 'Brother' Paul Verity, is a loose neo-Marxist, anti-fascist grouping which has maintained close ties with extreme left-wing groups in Eastern Europe. While it has standard communist elements in its programme – state ownership of all industrial production, state control of the unions and the labour force, withdrawal from NATO and all other Western-capitalist treaty obligations, and the introduction of a massive social welfare programme, it is also distinctly nationalistic in outlook, which is a measure of the Brother's strong personal influence on its politics. It too, for example, believes in keeping North Sea oil entirely British owned . . .

The bitter conclusion to Gregory's book, and one that he felt no need to revise, was that the CDA coalition of 'moderate, sensible men and women' had been too long in coming and had failed to stem the flood of industrial war and class and race hate. Against this sorry background, there was one additional destabilising factor which had removed the safety-valve from that society: the violence that had once thrived in Northern Ireland had anaesthetised the British public, through the media's constant sensationalising of dire events, to the extent that they had become totally apathetic and inoculated against violence and death. Politicians and the man in the street had both relied too long on 'the good sense of the British' to save them from tragedy. Now, according to Gregory's bitter analysis, it was almost too late, with Britain poised on the brink of catastrophe.

Four

T HEY WERE mainly identikit men, business executives, government officials, administrators, though there was a scattering of feminine leavening in the two or three immaculate women from, at a guess, the same dull professions. All had neat briefcases and carried copies of the *New York Times* or the *Wall Street Journal* or early editions of the *Washington Post*. No sign of the *Daily News* on this flight; no ordinary people, no students, tourists, shopkeepers, mistresses on the seven a.m. Eastern Airlines shuttle to Washington.

Max Gregory perched on a hard plastic bench into which someone had burned a series of neat holes with the end of a cigarette. He was irritated: irritated by the late arrival of his driver which had meant missing the first section of the shuttle, irritated by the ink smudge on his hands from reading the *New York Times*, irritated by the lead editorial which was preaching, as so often, with no solution to offer:

The trends that have bedevilled Britain since the Second World War have dramatically worsened. Only a short time ago, we, along with the American Irish community at large, were elated when Westminster at last brought relative peace to Ulster. But at what price. Now Britain is not only the sick man of Europe, it is itself critically divided. The benefits from North Sea oil have led neither to an increase in stability nor to economic prosperity but have been accompanied by vicious political turmoil. The left has marshalled the unions into an ever more powerfully militant and violent force, causing US investors to seek other less volatile areas in which to place capital.

The loudspeaker called the departure of the second section. Gregory folded the newspaper, picked up his briefcase and coat and edged into line. Slowly, with boarding pass in hand, he advanced up the sound-proofed mounting ramp and into the cramped plane. Settling himself at a window seat, with difficulty he re-opened the paper and forced himself to continue with the editorial. It was not that the *Times* line was wrong or particularly unbalanced, just full of empty rhetoric.

> The right-wing, even those less extreme than the camp-followers of the so-called 'Commander', calls for harsh totalitarian methods to deal with the strikes and lawlessness which their own policies encourage. Racism and the call for interment of the 'Enemies of the State' (a phrase increasingly used to describe any striker or demonstrator), these and the encouragement of paramilitary vigilante groups are strident parts of the political platform of the right. More dangerously, some senior military and police officers, frustrated in their attempts to control metropolitan hooliganism and faced with increasing sectarian violence in Scotland and Wales, are reported to be siding with extreme conservative leaders. On the left are the familiar neo-Marxist ideologues and their running dogs . . . such as we have seen so often elsewhere around the globe . . .

A large fat man in a rumpled blue-shot suit plunged into the insufficient seat beside Gregory, bulging the centre armrest and pressuring him even tighter against the window. 'Whoops,' he wheezed in a very English voice, 'shuttle planes ain't built for the big 'uns.'

Gregory responded with an imperceptible nod as he struggled but failed to regain his fair share of the seating. Arms pinned in front of him, he attempted to renegotiate the *Times* into a readable position but could not turn the pages and was again forced to face the offending editorial.

The State Department continues to hold that this is a domestic British matter . . . no direct concern of the US Administration . . . White House anxiety . . . there are dangers . . . Western Alliance . . . old and trusted ally . . . tragedy of great historical . . . dangers of intervention . . .

Eyes heavy, Gregory let his head drop back with the paper crumpled unhappily in his lap. The best of a bad start would be to sleep and dream of spacious executive jets. Cassover would have sent a plane if he had asked.

'I know you. You're Lou Gregory's brother.' The heavy voice in his right ear was unmistakably Yorkshire. Any other topic would have brought a derelict response aimed at killing any further attempt at conversation. As it was, Gregory turned his head as far as he could and came face to face with an uncertain smile and a fair quantity of bad breath.

'Yes, yes. Twins you were. Could hardly miss you, could I? Reddich . . . Jimmy Reddich. French horn. Off to join the Washington Symphony.'

'I . . . yes . . . Max Gregory.' They struggled to shake hands.

'How d'you do, Max . . . Saw you only once. That night, I'm afraid. Seems ages ago, but it can't be more'n a month . . . You came to pick Lou up. God, we all talked about how happy he was . . . Later that was, when we heard. We all liked Lou.'

'Yes.' Gregory gave up his contortionist's attempt to look at his companion. He had also given up the idea of sleep.

'Everyone liked Lou. Good, competent instrumentalist. That leg of his – he must have been in constant pain. But never heard him complain. How d'it happen?'

'Bad fall on ice. Multiple fracture.'

'He had the luck.' The fat man sighed into a brief silence. 'Wait a minute. You vanished, didn't you? Disappeared. They were looking for you. Said you had wiped out . . .' Gregory felt the huge bulk stirring uneasily beside him as memories were revived.

'Hey. Wait. They said you had shot . . . hey . . . wasn't that it ? God . . . Oh God.'

Gregory could feel the man staring at him. He could imagine the horror-struck face but did not turn to look and kept his eyes firmly on the clasp that held up the little collapsible tray in front of him. Maybe the man would move, would shout for the stewardess, would point a finger at a reputed mass-murderer. No such luck.

'Say . . . They deserved it. We all thought so. Musicians may not be the most . . . er . . . belligerent of people, but by God, what they did to Lou . . . It *was* you, wasn't it?'

'It depends what you mean.'

'No, no. Don't say anything. I don't want to know. But they did think . . .' He paused.

'Yes? Who thought?'

'Yes, yes. The police. Then Section Nine of the Security Squad interrogated us all, to find where you were. The leader, of the orchestra that is, he was closest to Lou. He went round to Lou's flat late the next day. In ruins. Someone had been right through it.'

'I heard.'

''Spect you pulled out . . . came over here quick. Can't blame you. Lou's death helped me make up my mind too, sure enough. Took up this Washington offer within the week, I did. I'm no quitter, but . . .'

'What was that about the Security Squad?' Gregory forced himself sideways in his seat in a renewed attempt to view the profile of the man beside him: a heavy, sweating face, unhealthy swinging jowls and no chin.

'I dunno. They talked to Frita – he was second trombone. He knew one of them. They were real "heavies". They told Frita there was some Russian link in the killing. You must know.'

'News to me. What else did they ask?'

'I dunno. A lot's happened since. I forget. I've been so thrown around by this move here. Different pace Stateside, don't you know. And I wasn't involved. Not me. It *is* almost a month now, isn't it?'

'Just over.'

'Just over, eh? Count the days, one does, with something like that. The heavies frightened the leader and Frita . . . They were throwing their weight around, you see.'

'You don't remember more about what they said about the Russians?'

'I don't . . . I don't remember nothing more. Nothing.'

The fat man dried up after that. Gregory tried to draw him further but the fat man sank deeper into his seat, spilling his bulk into ever greater overflow and was silent. It was only when they arrived at Washington and the fat man had, with much effort, levered himself out of his tortured seat, that he addressed Gregory again. 'Nice to meet . . . I mean . . . well I'm sorry . . . very sorry. We all liked Lou, you know. We really did.'

'This is the CBS News with Edward Airdale.' Almost the only watchable programme came on screen. How many times had the grand old man of American television retired as anchorman and then had to come back in response to the ratings battle and to public demand?

Gregory lay stretched out on his hotel bed, shoes off, shirt unbuttoned to the waist. To hell with Cassover, Auerbach, the lot of them. They had kept him waiting all day with an endless flow of excuses. 'Dr Auerbach is with the President . . .' 'Admiral Cassover is still at the NSC . . .' 'The President is at a Pentagon briefing.' The crisis this time apparently was that in China, over a million were now reported dead in the earthquake, the epicentre of which was in the Province of . . . where was it? Auerbach, Cassover and the President were working on how the US should respond to an unexpected Chinese request for massive American aid. In the middle of the morning the Secretary of State sent an assistant to Gregory's hotel to apologise in person. 'The Secretary of State is extremely sorry. He is looking forward to a full discussion with you later, after lunch . . .' Then came telephone calls: 'four o'clock . . .', 'six o'clock', 'seven o'clock'. 'Professor Gregory, you would be better to stay in Washington overnight if that isn't inconvenient.' 'Overnight . . .' To hell with them all.

His eyes narrowed. He needed a Scotch, but not quite yet. He sat up on the bed and, ignoring the television, picked his way listlessly through a bundle of intelligence reports he had brought with him. The trouble with the CIA was that their UK Filter Unit was ineffective and the most basic intelligence material came through to the Institute unchecked. Gregory had brought some examples with him to take up with Cassover if time allowed.

Report CZ 991/8/84: Riot gear for police. After nine months' debate, traditional 'Bobby' helmet finally abandoned in favour of Intermex Stormtroop Model K, complete with shatter-proof vizor and neck-protector. Antimolotov suiting and riot guns firing rubber chain now issued all, repeat all, metropolitan forces . . .

Report CZ 821/9/84: Water contamination. Allegations of deliberate left-wing depurification of Merseyside drinking-water supplies have been vehemently denied by spokesman for Waterworkers' Union . . .

Report CZ 1012/9/84: Food convoys. Reappraisal of convoy security has been called for following hijacking of five lorries and contents in East London dock area, Saturday night. Food stocks and emergency medical supplies in the area are consequently running drastically low. On the black market most commodities are, by contrast, easily available. No serious attempts by metropolitan authorities to deal with illegal food dealing have been reported.

In the verbatim series of foreign press coverage of the British crisis, Gregory turned to select one with a Moscow dateline.

Following from CIA for onpass Gregory Institute: Text of *Pravda* article dated today Thursday, January 20: 'The Soviet Politbureau rejects allegations emanating from

Washington and Bonn that they have in any way involved themselves in the struggle by the working-class peoples of the United Kingdom against the resurgence of fascism in that country. The Soviet people deplore attempts to suggest that it has financed the efforts of the peace-loving People's Socialist Coalition, though it will continue, as must all those involved in the fight against neo-colonialism, imperialism and fascism, to give moral support where it can. Additionally, it condemns the backing being given, both in money and weapons, by international capitalism to the so-called 'Commander' and his storm-trooper thugs of the UAM. It warns those responsible for fuelling the hatred and the attacks on the British working classes that the Soviet Union cannot and will not stand idly by and watch neo-nazism and warmongering capitalism reassert itself. The Government of Prime Minister Harold Hunt must use all the power at its disposal to destroy the evil of fascism before it is itself destroyed . . .

Gregory threw the reports back on top of his open briefcase and allowed his thoughts to wander. He had a most reliable address to follow up in Georgetown. *There* was a lady who had never failed him. Soon he might . . . His attention moved back to the television screen where CBS, still unaware that the US had been asked for aid, gave one minute thirty seconds of their evening news to the Chinese earthquake. In global terms it was important, otherwise they wouldn't have given it ninety seconds and put it as first foreign item. The standard piece on the developing world energy crisis took the next place, then came a hotel fire in Las Vegas. After the ads came Britain. Edward Airdale, everyone's favourite grandfather with his slanting, kindly eyes and a microphone buttonholed neatly on his tie, was talking in a sad, almost English voice, about a great old country gone mad. The Britain that 'had lost an Empire . . .' now seemed totally intent on 'weaving its own shroud. The great mass of sensible British people were sitting around with minds like wool, playing or watching cricket and saying "oh dear" while the mother of democracies burned around them.' Fine, homespun political analysis, Gregory thought as he lay on his bed, watching the newscaster shed earnest tears over Britain on the brink. 'And today brought further reports of conflict in that decaying society, as Mark Rudin reports from London,' said Airdale wisely.

Gregory weakened, got up from the bed, poured himself the needed drink and settled back to watch the film which was of bodies lined up on some anonymous rain-soaked London street. Behind the corpses the camera picked out a group of soldiers in riot gear and helmets, with the perspex face shields pushed back so that they could have a smoke and a chat. Not one of them was paying any attention as a little old lady in black pulled and turned her way along the neat line of bodies that lay stretched out waiting to be identified. The CBS cameraman with astute, award-winning skill, picked out the old lady holding back her tears, the soldiers smoking and the corpses on the wet tarmac. Then the camera panned up to take in the face of Big Ben.

The telephone rang. Gregory picked it up, listened, grunted, then replaced the receiver. He got up, showered, changed his shirt and put on a suit and tie for the late night summons.

'And that's the way it is this Thursday, January 20. This is Edward Airdale for CBS News. Good night.' Gregory leaned over and pressed the button on the set. The screen went blank.

Five

THEY STOOD marshalled on the terrace outside the french windows. 'OK. Let's get this charade over quick,' growled Auerbach. A personal adviser nodded obediently, two Secret Servicemen stood aside and the Secretary of State pushed his way into the Oval Office without knocking. Gregory followed, shook hands with the President who stood smiling by the door, then moved to his allotted seat with his back to those famous bulletproof windows that produced, by repute, such a curiously distorted view of the wider world beyond.

Besides Gregory there were seven other people in the office. Three were senior White House or State Department aides, one was a hyper-attractive stenographer, one Admiral Hugh Cassover, Director of the CIA, and one the Secretary of State, Dr Frank Auerbach. The last man, and by any account the least gifted of them all, was the stooped, wispish figure who was the President of the United States of America. Contrary to conventional wisdom about how presidents act and power is manipulated, none of the men in the room were at his bidding. Rather it was that the President had had his evening spoiled by the demand for this meeting, because his advisers wished to use him and his authority. He was puck, they had the sticks, and it was now a matter of alliances, teamwork and tactics into which net he was finally homed. But the ceremonial play-acting that is part of every nation's decision-taking process had first to be followed through.

'I have twenty minutes,' said the President with a brief demonstration of authority, as he swung himself round behind his desk to face his visitors. No one had ever denied the *Washington Post* story which had appeared when the President first took up office: that his policy making had begun with a directive that his swivel chair should be specially built-up to give him a throne-like stature over those who would sit around him. That the President needed every available stage prop was a view that Gregory shared as he watched and wondered, yet again, at how such a physically nondescript man, with all his inadequacies on constant public display, could end up as the nation's Chief Executive.

'Twenty minutes till bed-time. My grandchildren won't forgive me if I don't say good night to them.' The skin on the President's face creased until the eyes almost disappeared. The result was the famous smile which, through the long presidential campaign, had hidden from the electorate the dull incompetence of the real man within.

'Ten minutes is all Britain's worth right now,' responded the Secretary of State with a matching leer that revealed much more than the line of uneven, tobacco-stained teeth. Gregory had to force himself to look at the speaker who sat in the place of honour on the right of the President. Under an angry turbulence of red hair that was every political cartoonist's joy, Dr Auerbach had always given Gregory the impression of being both devious and menacing. They had known and disliked each other at Yale many years earlier when Auerbach was Dean of Political Studies. Now, with academic life behind him, Auerbach had acquired the State Department, which, with a weak president like the present one, left him with almost absolute power in the making of American foreign policy.

The President beamed around the room, then, speaking from notes, launched himself into a trite little speech. 'Professor Gregory, as you know, we, the US Administration, wish to do everything in our power to help the United Kingdom to recover, both politically and economically. It is necessary not only for the future of Western defence and stability but also, dare I say, Professor, for the future of civilisation itself. That is why the Administration and particularly the CIA have underwritten your, our, common research project. It is one that we value greatly as an extension of the governmental process of this great nation of ours. I, er . . . hope and trust . . . ,' the President faltered, ' . . . that we can continue to work closely on this project for our . . . er . . . mutual benefit and for that . . . er . . . of society at large. Er . . . Frank, over to you.' The President sat back, a contented look on his face at a job well done, a case well put.

Auerbach leaned forward in his chair. 'Thank you, Mr President,' he said, then turned and addressed Gregory. 'Cards on the table, Professor. The President is, on CIA advice, considering asking you to step up your operation in the UK. That's why you were asked here today. Against State Department advice, CIA propose that they should double the amount of sponsorship money available to the Gregory Institute. Your aim from now on would not just be to analyse the British predicament and its energy resources, but to help find solutions. I, with respect, believe that that is the Administration's job, not yours.'

'Fact is, things are getting worse. We need all the expert help we can buy from . . .' At the interruption, Dr Auerbach turned irritably to focus on the uncertain figure of Admiral Cassover. The CIA Director's reputation was coloured by his habits. One was that he seemed incapable of finishing a sentence, as if he wished to keep his audience guessing at his intentions. Another was that Cassover would polish his bald pate rapidly with the flat of his right hand as he spoke, both trade marks of a man who had been selected for his patent honesty to become head of the Augean stables that were still the core of the intelligence community of the United States of America. The *Washington Post* had called him a big kindly frontman, the former war hero and football champion who was still bull-chested enough to carry his many rows of military decorations with conviction. The other story was that he had been appointed with Auerbach's specific blessing. A not over-brilliant director for the CIA would mean that Langley would always come second in the traditional battle with the Special Services Section of the State Department.

'Agreed,' Auerbach responded. His eyes darted from person to person around the room as he weighed up who was with him and who against. He was a man who lived by conflict, and if it did not exist he created it. 'Agreed,' he repeated, in a tone that suggested the precise opposite. 'No one's disputing you, Admiral. Your reports tally exactly with those of State Department.'

'The same sources . . . ours, though State Department tends not to acknowledge the fact.' This time Cassover made sure everyone got the whole message.

'Now then, tut, tut,' said the President, as if already with his grandchildren.

'We're working together very closely, Mr President,' said Dr Auerbach, shifting his style to one of sweet reason. 'What we're here to discuss, the Admiral will remember, is what conclusion we may draw from the British situation, and how Professor Gregory and his Institute may be able to help with solutions. We're agreed it's getting worse, but does it matter? Why does the state of Britain matter to the US of A?'

'It matters a great deal to us. We felt we should disturb your evening, Mr President, because . . .' Cassover hesitated, '. . . race riots, violent picketing, neo-fascist parades supported by the police, all this, taken together, poses a threat to our economic and political standing in Western Europe, the balance of power, NATO defence capabilities and so on. Then take the oil factor; Professor Gregory's already working for us on a specific project on oil reserves. As one of the most prominent experts on the British political mood he believes we have to act now . . . He shares my belief that we can't just . . .' As his words dried up Cassover picked up his folder of briefs with a ball-player's huge hand and waved it in the empty air in front of him.

'We could indeed just.' Auerbach's red hair bobbed up and down aggressively as he stressed the last word. 'We could do lots of things or nothing. We could send in the Sixth Fleet. We could get all hot under the collar and tell Prime Minister Hunt to get a grip. Ask him to issue sten guns to his wonderful police.'

'The police are all armed these days,' Gregory interjected. As soon as he spoke he realised it was a mistake. The last thing these people wanted was more facts. Auerbach and Cassover stared at him with equal distaste.

'A message, a personal message from you Mr President, from you to the Prime Minister, would certainly strengthen his resolve.' Cassover pressed ahead undaunted. 'We have also considered sponsoring a UN resolution calling for a United Nations force to help in metropolitan riot control, which would take one problem off Hunt's back. Another major financial loan could help the economy get going once again. All these options are worth urgent consideration.'

'The answer to these is no, no and no,' interrupted Auerbach, showing increasing irritation. 'The first, with respect, Mr President, would do no good. I'm sure poor Harold Hunt would appreciate the gesture, but you'd be wasting your time. And as for the hoary old idea of a UN force it would be Cyprus or Korea all over again. A thankless task, with us Americans taking all the burden and we'd have a helluva hard job keeping the Russians out. It would most likely give the Kremlin a toe-hold in Western Europe and more ammo for their "human-rights-is-also-a-western-issue" line. It's like it was with Ireland. The Paddys kept on killing each other whatever we did since they had centuries of habit to live up to and it was only when they decided for themselves that enough was enough that they came to their senses. As for the Admiral's loan idea: with the amount of good money we've poured after bad, quite apart from what Treasury would say . . .' Auerbach paused and turned to face Gregory. 'The Professor is a considerable expert on the UK. Does he go along with this? Does he really see any of that crap making a jot of difference?'

Gregory saw that he was being set a trap and began cautiously. 'With other world sources so uncertain, North Sea oil supplies are increasingly important. If we sit back and let Britain pull itself to pieces, who's going to control access?' To emphasise his point he brought the flat of his hand down on the arm of his chair with more force than he intended.

'Why not?' responded Auerbach, with a suitably withering look. The Secretary of State had been brought up on Kissinger's doctrine of European inconsequence; he was now about to add his own touch of malice. 'Precisely why not, Professor Gregory? The multinational oil companies will continue to get it out to us even if Britain does go up in flames. So why does Britain really matter to the US? We don't need their defence capability, such as they have left after using it in riot control, fighting fires and delivering groceries when everyone's on strike. The situation's not even affecting our trade. We're selling as much to them as we've ever done.'

'Leaving aside oil, Secretary of State, a further deterioration could, as Admiral Cassover said, affect the whole European balance of power. With Britain in ruins, there's a gaping hole in the Euopean end of the Atlantic Alliance. Don't you think the Russians would exploit that just as much?' answered Gregory, with matching ice in his voice.

'Right,' broke in Cassover. 'Professor Gregory has a real grasp of . . .'

'Professor Gregory – you're British, aren't you?' asked Auerbach, carefully reacting to the Cassover–Gregory line-up. 'Balance of power' was a phrase which the President might think he understood.

'I'm an American citizen,' said Gregory. He knew at once what was coming.

'But born, raised and educated in Britain. Fifteen years here in the States, isn't it, Professor? America's gain; Britain's loss. We all agree. And your brother . . . That was very sad. Very sad. You know from experience about the rule of the hard-hearted thug, Professor. You remember, Mr President, about the Professor's brother. The Professor is an unrivalled expert on the British political situation and he mustn't let his recent tragic loss affect his judgement as to what to do about it.'

The President took a point that he could scarcely have missed. 'Yes indeed. Very sad . . . Now, I think,' he said, 'it's the youngsters' bed-time. If there's nothing else, gentlemen, I'd better be going. My grandchildren are very demanding, you know.'

The President stood up and so did everyone else. Cassover looked as if he was about to explode but then thought better of it. Gregory considered telling the President the facts about his brother's death, and of his growing convictions that he had been the real target of the thugs because his work for the CIA had leaked, but he too controlled himself. Explanations achieved little when the damage was done. He would also swallow his anger at Auerbach's malicious suggestion that he lacked impartiality.

Six

AUERBACH was already over an hour late for the meeting but this time Gregory had Cassover for company as they sat waiting in the Secretary of State's ante-room at the State Department. Aides and secretaries flitted in from time to time to ensure a plentiful supply of coffee.

'He always keep you waiting like this?'

'When he's with the President. China again. I should be at my desk working on it too.' Cassover seemed remarkably composed despite the delay but even he kept glancing at his watch.

'You accept it?' Gregory queried.

'Being kept waiting? . . . This time, yes. Britain's more important in the long run. Auerbach knows I want something from him, so he can afford to be a bit late.'

'What game was he playing last night? One moment he was totally anti your proposal, down-playing the British crisis generally, and the next he appeared to give in to my getting more involved.'

'Game-playing, as you say. Auerbach thrives on antagonisms. But he knows he's lost this round.' Cassover continued to demonstrate a remarkable degree of resignation.

'What's that?'

'Better wait till he tells you, Max; it's part of my deal with him. You see, he's annoyed, since generally his first objective is to get the President to rubber-stamp his blank cheques, if you see what I mean.'

'I don't see.'

'Auerbach believes that it's better to keep detail away from the President, that it just confuses the mind of the Chief

Executive. So he was mad as hell at me for setting up the meeting with you. We should have fixed everything first and told the President afterwards.'

'What's the "everything"?'

There was a long pause. At the end of it Cassover ignored Gregory's question and asked another. 'You're planning to go to London soon?'

'Tuesday. I want to get the oil project over and done. You're footing the bill, so we've both got an interest in seeing an early finish. And even with your global preoccupations you wouldn't expect me to forget Lou. I can't accept not knowing who did it and why.'

'I suppose,' Cassover grunted. 'But better to wait till the London police have cooled off looking for you, Max. We're not that desperate for the oil project. A few more weeks and . . . Any case, CIA Head of London Station is against any idea of you returning now. He says you'd be asking for a heap of trouble.' He stood up and walked over to where a silver tray of drinks lay on top of a glass-fronted bookcase. 'What's yours?'

'Not now, Admiral. Too early.'

'Clear head for Auerbach? Right you are. But I will. It's nearly mid-day.' With inordinate care he mixed himself a very dry Martini, then went on: 'You'd be foolish. Head of Station can't guarantee to protect you all the time once you're there . . .'

'Why should I expect him to?'

'You're valuable . . . to us, that's why. Let the situation settle a bit more.'

'If it does that, it'll give the police more time on their hands to look for me. But it won't. It's going to get worse, a lot worse. I have to see people in the Ministry of Energy and elsewhere in Whitehall who simply won't be there once London finally starts burning up.'

'We'll see . . .' Cassover broke off as irritation at last began to show through. 'Where the hell is Auerbach? I haven't got all day.'

'Nor have I,' said Gregory, 'but that's the way it's been these last twenty-four hours.'

An aide slipped into the room on cue. 'Secretary of State's on the way over from the White House, Admiral. He's sorry to have kept you.'

'Sure, sure,' said Cassover, giving an extra polish to his pate with the flat of his hand. 'Sure he is.'

When the aide eased back out of the ante-room, Gregory stood up and went to join the Admiral by the drinks tray. 'I know your people have other things to do,' he said. 'But have they dug up anything more?'

'Oh, yes, your brother. I . . . say, I thought I'd tell you later what we'd found.' Cassover paused.

'Kind of you to think about it.'

'I didn't mean that,' the response was soft. 'I don't joke about death. After years in the navy I realise it's the only unfunny part.'

'So?'

'There's increasing evidence that they *were* after you that night . . .'

'I said that from the start.'

'Wait a minute. At first Head of CIA London Station didn't listen when you suggested it wasn't a mugging.'

'He was sympathetic and sceptical. Equal doses. He didn't hear what those thugs in grey said, so I couldn't blame him. Why should anyone be after me just because you're sponsoring my project? Should Head of London Station think different?'

'He does now.'

'Why?'

'A CIA planning paper got picked up . . . lost if you like. We still don't know who took it or when, but it went all right. Head of London himself discovered the day after you left that it hadn't been logged out of Registry; it just wasn't there. I was angry about that.'

'Planning paper? On what?'

'You.'

'I see. But I've always assumed the British Government knew about my present . . . that I was working for the CIA. That's hardly a death licence, even today.'

'Not the British.'

'Who then?'

'The Kremlin.'

'The Kremlin. So why the hell should they be upset with me. They've probably known about the oil project for months.'

'Sure they have.'

'For Christ sake, Admiral. What are you on about? The men that got Lou were the Commander's UAM thugs.'

'Or dressed to look like them.'

'Go on.' Gregory stood stock still, watching the other man intently.

'There's an extremist Marxist hit-squad. We've identified a number of them . . .'

'Who?'

'It's not the who you should be interested in, it's the why.' Carrying his martini, Cassover moved away from the drinks cabinet towards a window.

'Is that meant to be a lead to what the President said about me and London?' Gregory was about to explode at the way the Admiral was playing him, but at that moment the State Department aide burst into the ante-room again. He was somewhat out of breath. 'The Secretary of State has arrived. He'll see you both now, Admiral . . . Professor . . .?'

'Coming right in,' said Cassover. Then he paused. 'I'll let Auerbach tell you, Max.'

The three men sat slung in deep leather and steel easy chairs at one end of the office. At the other end, two of Auerbach's assistants were poised on hard upright chairs taking notes.

'Really sorry,' repeated the Secretary of State for the third or fourth time. The sentiment did not improve with repetition. 'OK, let's get on. Now you tell me how you think this British thing really is . . . No, wait.' He turned to one of his men.

'Send a wire. For Jack, for the Ambassador in Moscow. Tell him to lay it hard on the line there that the amount of aid we're giving China changes nothing. OK? Nothing. Straight, good, old out-of-the-bottom-of-our-star-spangled-hearts charity . . . OK? Tell the Embassy to lay that on as thick as they like. We don't have no political motivations; just charity. If the Kremlin believe that they'll believe anything. But at least because we've explained it to them nicely, they'll wipe their tears and feel a bit better.'

As one of the secretaries left to send the wire, Auerbach settled back in his chair, and, pulling back his lips in his version of a smile, revealed the uneven yellowed teeth. 'Now where were we? Oh . . . Oh yes, Max. Britain, that was it.'

Gregory sat stone-faced at the little show of power-politics that, he suspected, had been put on at least in part for his benefit. Auerbach was telling him to set the British problem in context or he'd be knocked into place. That was Auerbach's style.

'Yes. First, let's have your current analysis, what you want me to hear. And, sorry Max, but if you can wrap it into the next ten minutes, say fifteen, so much the better. There just ain't enough time in a day.'

Gregory looked at Cassover and bit back his temper. He was being provoked and tested, but knowing Auerbach's style there must be a reason for it. That was the way the Secretary of State operated and Gregory knew he had to play the game all the way. So he went through the British predicament again from lesson one, explaining the idealism that led to the extreme left's drive to bring about a neo-communist state, the centre-moderate's failures, and the fortification of the right-wing backlash which had increasingly moulded itself on the Mosleyite black-shirts of the thirties.

Auerbach stirred in his chair. 'OK, OK, Max. Junior High School stuff. That's for the record.' He waved in the direction of his staff man. 'My boy there has got it all down for you. Now let's get on.'

Gregory remained calm, playing it long and presenting his

case in an unusually pedestrian way in an attempt to draw Auerbach, realising that, as usual, personalities and the conflicts between them were about to cause more decisions to be taken or not to be taken than the facts allowed.

'We went through all that with the President last night. Where's the advance?' Auerbach interrupted.

'The advance is that the situation's got worse.'

'I know that too. I read the telegrams.'

'My interpretation of it has changed.'

'Aha! It has, has it? The news hadn't reached me.'

Gregory bit his lip and bypassed the sarcasm. 'Secretary of State, I believe that the British Government would have been able to hold the situation steady and our oil supplies and other interests would be safeguarded if only . . .'

'The basic good sense of the Brits, eh? The sort of inherited wisdom and justice that made you all what you are, Max?'

'Don't push him, Secretary of State,' broke in Cassover.

'Professor Gregory doesn't usually worry about things like that. Not known for his tolerance either. Nor for being so long-winded.'

'All right, Secretary of State,' Gregory snapped. 'The crisis would not have escalated without someone or some group manipulating events, making sure compromise isn't reached, precipitating new riots when things start going well. Anything to ensure Harold Hunt gets nowhere.'

'Aha, that's the nub, is it? But Harold Hunt will never get anywhere. You know he hasn't the intelligence to see he's a fool.'

'We can agree on that. But it's not just him. There are sufficient well-meaning men around him.'

'Well-meaning never solved problems, particularly Britain's sort.'

'Street leaders of both sides are being used. Some caucus, possibly inside the the British Establishment but much more likely abroad, is working hard to bring Britain to the brink.'

'You're not calling it an invisible hand?'

'I might even call it that. If I were forced to bet, I'd say it was a classic case of someone plotting chaos to be followed by the rule of the strong man.'

'Clever. Who's your culprit?' Auerbach paused and threw a glance at the Admiral.

'It could be one of Britain's former European Common Market partners. The Franco-German Alliance could, for example, do with the oil and with picking up some of Britain's traditional trading areas.'

'No way, Professor. The French and the Germans have their hands full with their own internal security problems quite apart from trying to keep the sad remains of the Common Market together. The Italians have a collapsed economy and about as much street anarchy as Britain. As for the Dutch and the Belgians, well now they've linked up with the Scandinavian Free Trade Area they have a bit more stability, but that crowd are all too nice . . .'

'OK. The Russians it is, though by and large they've sided with the Brother's People's Socialist Coalition, and have given them a lot of money if not weapons.'

'Got it second time round, Max. As far as the US of A is concerned, the hand, as always, is a Soviet one. They're the only ones who would really benefit in the long run from British disunity, even more than they could ever do by backing the Brother. He's too much of a patriot.'

'I'm going over Tuesday. If I find out, I'll drop you a postcard.'

'You go nowhere. If you do you won't come back, because it'll be you, not your brother, next time.'

'Look, I've had this out with the Admiral already.' Gregory began to lose his control. 'I'm doing this research project for the CIA, plain and simple, like dozens of think-tank analysts have before me. Liberals here may still call that a sin but it's hardly big news in Britain any more, nor likely to worry the Russians out of their sleep.'

'Then you tell me why your brother died, why the people

who got him wanted you? Go on, tell me,' prodded Auerbach relentlessly.

'Those papers that got lost . . .' Cassover began to speak, then looked at Auerbach and stopped in mid-sentence.

'Tell me about them, Secretary of State,' Gregory looked at the two men. On top of the President's remark there was something coming he did not like. Auerbach was grimacing and even Cassover wasn't acting to form.

'They set out precisely what the CIA had in mind for you, which was nothing directly to do with your oil work. What you just said about the crisis being manipulated . . .' Auerbach edged into a more comfortable position in his chair, the yellow leer still clamped across his face.

'Go on,' Gregory could feel a trap closing round him.

'We thought that if the Kremlin was to try that game we would want to react to it hard and fast.'

'And?'

There was a pause, then Auerbach hissed. 'I am to inform you that, whatever my views, the President has personally chosen you as his top-level liaison man in London.'

'The US Ambassador . . . You have . . .'

'Behind the scenes, of course. The Ambassador . . . not a great intellect . . . a member of the party faithful and of course we can't remove him right now, can we? But Premier Hunt's not at all impressed by him and has long been complaining to us about the lack of high-level liaison between us. So His Excellency stays, but as front man. As for me, well you might as well know that I've been against the project, but I'll have to live with it, since that's the way it's going to be. You, Professor Max Gregory, are the loyal Brit come home in your country's time of need. You're the President's personal link with, or if he doesn't go along with it, against Hunt. You can have what additional staff and money you need – within reason, from CIA sources.'

'I want to think about it.'

'That's a luxury you can't afford, Max; on that the Admiral

57

and I are in total agreement. And the President goes along with the Admiral's proposal. He had to show you to him first. For the record, you understand. It's his decision after all.' He paused and grinned. 'Not Tuesday, but soon, very soon, Max, you go to London. You're the key from now on. As you said yourself, America can't let Britain go to pieces, not in the last resort. With the balance of power and all that, if there's a political vacuum, then by God the United States must be ready to fill it.'

Gregory stared at each man in turn. They both looked back at him in their separate ways.

Seven

OVER THE next five weeks Britain followed much the same course except that every day things got a little worse. To the staff of London's Inter-Continental Hotel, now mainly British since the Spaniards and Italians had moved on to happier climes, the American correspondents were vultures. They sat around the bar waiting to pick at the carrion of the day's events and turn it into copy. They were war correspondents come to observe the process of one more nation's slide into tragedy, having over the last year largely replaced the desk-bound bureau boys who had gone on, like the waiters, to the relative tranquillity of Paris, Bonn and Rome. They were hard men, seen-it-all veterans of Saigon, Beirut, Tehran, Warsaw and now London. They were waiting for the kill, perched on stools along the bar of their latest Inter-Continental, speculating on how long it would be till this city too was burned and bombed into the ground. Until that day, until they scrambled and fought on to the last USAF plane out, the bar would be their club, the clearing house for their stories.

The doyen of the little group was Dan Lateman of AP, fifty-ish, eyes like little blood-stained pools in a lined white face. He'd been held by the Vietcong, beaten up by the Ayatollah's men in Tehran, thrown out of Warsaw by the Russians after the invasion, and a week ago had had shots fired at him in a Bayswater Street just as he was leaving from an interview with the Commander. Beside him, balanced on a black-topped bar stool sat Zarnuk; no one called him by his christian name, even if they knew it. Zarnuk of the *Washington*

Post, lips stained brown with nicotine, sat chewing on the shreds of a dead cigar. A Pulitzer prize lay somewhere in his past; something to do with China, or was it an interview with Nasser? Next on the row of perches was Roly Smith, unshaven, unwashed and crumpled, drinking himself into an early trip to the crematorium with a salary from *Time Inc*. And last, a little apart as always and the only one of them to have stayed on in London from before, was Andrei Jameson from the *Chicago Herald Tribune*. He had been in London so long that his accent was imperceptible and his three-piece suits unmistakable. Two scotches, one very large martini and a brandy and soda were arranged in front of them.

They were men that talked, as they always talked, in shorthand, loaded with nick-names unknown outside the clique, a checkerboard of unpolished phrases. They'd seen a lot of the same things that day as every day: dead on the streets, the latest TV appeal for calm by the Prime Minister, another march by some group or other towards the barbed-wire barriers that encircled Whitehall and Westminster. Roly had had a *Time* photographer with him: great shots of armed soldiers guarding the gutted Treasury building at the corner of Parliament Square; of the Reverend 'Mac' MacNair, the fundamentalist cleric who was one of the Commander's deputies, haranguing a crowd in Hyde Park; of the body of a Pakistani who had been tarred, feathered and set alight in Brixton; of a group of young 'soviets' at a political rally in Canning Town. Their moving, pithy stories were filed and now they could relax.

Lateman was doing the talking. As usual he was ahead of the game and could afford to tell them what extra copy he had. He had already wired his poignant exclusive interview with Harold Hunt. The Prime Minister had begun reasonably confident and poised, his remarks larded with traditional clichés about the common sense of the British, and that this was just a temporary moment of insanity in the great pattern of their history. 'When the storm dies,' he went on, 'the seas will be calm again', and Lateman had to force himself not to smile. Overall, the Prime Minister appeared self-assured, despite the recent attempts on his life.

Then Lateman had interrupted to ask about the other, successful assassination, that of the Minister of Defence who had been blown to pieces by a car bomb some weeks earlier. 'Why had he been a particular target?' Lateman asked. Mention of the murder had had a marked trigger-effect as the Prime Minister had fought to retain his self-control. Then, suddenly, it all came pouring out, with the journalist scribbling it down as hard as he could. His colleagues listened as Lateman read, from shorthand notes, his resultant assessment of the man and his character.

Hunt had from the start demonstrated that, deep down, he was not a complete fool. A politician of the old school, he had grown up in the right of the Labour Party before joining the Social Democrats in 1981. He retained a deep belief in democracy and in the House of Commons, and had long feared the attractions that the extremes of the political spectrum offered the electorate. His disillusionment with the system had led him to leave politics for some time, only to re-emerge within the last year to try to pull his CDA coalition together into some sort of cohesive force. To Lateman, Hunt's weaknesses were obvious: a personal lack of any ability to appeal to the public at large, and an equal lack of understanding that the old system of party loyalties had gone for ever. Hunt had even admitted to Lateman that he considered the Commander as a democrat gone wrong, a man with a distinguished military career behind him, who had always declared himself a strong British nationalist, rather than a fascist. He was someone, Hunt argued, who had simply gone on from where Enoch Powell had left off, and who had appreciated the attractions of 'ethnic Britons right or wrong' slogans and an increasingly virulent anti-communism. In present circumstances it was hard for anyone to argue against tough law-and-order measures, something the Commander said he stood for even though his own street politics created the very conditions in which civil order was most needed.

'OK. So?' Lateman's monologue was interrupted by Zarnuk of the *Post*. 'Another homespun analysis from the man behind the misery. What does it do except highlight Hunt's lack of leadership?'

'No praise from me,' said Lateman in a low voice. 'But I got one of the best off-the-record briefings ever. Right down to who's with whom in Cabinet. The Social Services Secretary . . . well, Hunt as good as said he's a pinko. The Home Secretary on the other wing is all for internment of left-wing leaders . . .'

'The Home Secretary's been after that for a while,' interjected Jameson. 'He's buddy-buddies with the Commander and has secret daily meetings with the United Action Movement Executive.'

'That's as maybe,' Lateman went on. 'Then Hunt had me listening to his theories as to who's behind it. He thinks it's all following a pattern.'

'Conspiracy of chaos? Anarchists perhaps?' asked Jameson cynically.

'Wrong . . . You know what Hunt thinks? He thinks there's a deliberate policy by the Soviets to keep things on the boil, wrecking things every time it looks as if he's having some success, an extreme Marxist action group pulling the rug away just when the Commander and the Brother feel like talking. D'you know, Hunt told me that just a few weeks ago both sides met secretly under his auspices on a navy ship. The Defence Secretary was the link man who pulled it all together. He was emerging as one of the stronger characters in the CDA coalition, and if it was chaos people wanted then he was the best man to waste. It looked as if the Minister had an agreement at least to call off the street violence, and both sides said they'd meet again. That was the night the Commander's ADC was maimed – Major what's-his-name, you remember? That, and blowing up the Defence Secretary, killed talks dead.'

'And?' asked Zarnuk after a pause.

'Hunt told me that both sides assured him they had kept

their word. The murder wasn't the Brother's nor the Commander's doing, and Hunt believed them.'

'A third group?'

'The Soviets – a Kremlin hit-squad.'

'Why the hell?'

'Standard Soviet ploy: divide and rule. They learnt it from the builder of the British Empire.'

'But surely,' asked Jameson, 'Hunt accepts that Moscow is right behind the Brother and his People's Socialist Coalition?'

'Too simple for Hunt,' replied Lateman. 'And I agree with him. The Kremlin never puts all its eggs in one basket and they're not a hundred per cent sure that the Brother *is* their man. He's too much of a loner that guy, and when the revolution comes, the last thing the Russkies want is a man with a mind of his own . . .'

There was a long pause, then Roly Smith's blurred voice boomed out: 'OK fellas. Another round and this time it's on me.'

'Good for you, Roly,' said Zarnuk.

An hour later, they were still there. They had watched the ITN headlines on the television set mounted at the corner of the bar. With the exception of a couple of girls chatting to the barman, no one came near them. The girls were on the wait for some late pick-up, some wayward American or Arab businessman still in London trying to get his money out before the end, and they knew it would be fruitless to approach these newsmen.

Andrei Jameson began talking but if the others were listening, they did not show it. Not that Jameson minded. He was rehearsing aloud what chapter two of the book he was writing on his life in Britain would say.

'In coping with the crisis,' he mused, 'the media themselves have gradually become more and more polarised. The PSC and the left are supported by a host of badly printed, party-financed fly-sheets which have given up any pretence of neutrality. Supporters of the Commander's UAM can, on the other hand, buy one or two of the former "quality" news-papers and upper-class tabloids which give the extreme right a well-produced and well-financed media platform. Rumbling along in the middle, the BBC and a tiny number of middle-of-the-road newspapers still claim to speak for reason and impartiality, but given the pressures on them by their own staffs, who swing to side either with the UAM or the PSC, they too are subjected to the veto of the extremes quite apart from the censorship which the Hunt Government also tries to impose on the distribution of all news.'

'Great stuff,' muttered Roly incoherently. 'Deathless effing . . . prose. Long live the freedom of the . . .'

'I remember,' Jameson went on, oblivious, eyes half-closed, 'it was only last summer I felt that they . . . the British, had already come to the brink. I was at Lords. That's a cricket ground and I'd been invited to watch something called the Second Test Match – the night before the Australians pulled out when their hotel was bombed. I was studying the crowd mainly, for cricket isn't something for a healthy man to watch. A big crowd: old men in regimental ties, blazers and moustaches; young men in open-necked shirts, all of them intent on the slowest of games. Did you ever read that article I wrote on cricket? It came out as a *Newsweek* essay – Roly, you should remember – well, maybe not just now you wouldn't. I wrote about the tedious boring incomprehensibility of it all, the soporific normality. Well, that's the way it was that last day of Test Match Cricket. I wonder if it'll ever come back. They don't play much cricket now . . . All these people, their minds like cotton wool, watching the world's most lifeless game, the sleeping-pill of the sporting life. They clapped and drank from hip flasks and people went in and were out and there were ducks and no-balls and tea and legs before and long stops and no one seemed to notice the police in steel helmets everywhere and the observation post on top of the clubhouse and the guards with SMG's. I thought for a moment that here was something that was strong and unflappable in the British way of life. Then I saw the police pulping some would-be

64

troublemaker with their truncheons. No one took much notice since some batsman was coming up for his century. It was the epitome of fiddling while the world burned around them. Riots, revolution, strikes, murders and what's happening in the Second Test. I realised that these people would be over the brink before they knew it and that even then most of them wouldn't notice. It was at that moment I knew it could, it would happen here, just then at Lords.'

Roly spilled his drink down his shirt-front and tried to wipe it away with a clumsy hand. There was a long silence, with Zarnuk staring into space; unmoving. Then slowly he began clapping. The short burst of sound echoed down the emptiness of the bar. Lateman laughed: Jameson turned on his stool, surprised and maybe a little hurt. The girls stood up together at the far end of the bar, kissed the barman and left without a glance at the gentlemen of the press.

After another silence Dan Lateman spoke. He measured his words. 'Odd little lead out of Washington DC, from my own personal "deep throat" at Langley. Maybe you guys can help. You know whom I mean by Max Gregory? Gregory Institute, New York. Now why's he coming here? What's bringing him to London town? Like tonight?'

Zarnuk, Jameson and even Roly Smith turned on their bar stools. Lateman had their attention.

Eight

DAN LATEMAN was, as usual, well informed. Professor Max Gregory, in his as yet unannounced new role as Special Envoy of the President of the United States, arrived in London on a much delayed Pan Am flight at eleven ten p.m. that same evening, Tuesday, March 1. The customs and immigration officers were on strike and only a handful of senior men were on duty at Heathrow, and while Gregory had hoped to avoid the VIP treatment, the lateness of the hour and the unrelieved gloom of the badly lit building made him grateful when a CIA liaison officer appeared and swept him through all the formalities unchecked.

'Head of London Station apologises for not coming out to meet you himself. Another US businessman kidnapped in Manchester. He's got his hands full negotiating with the terrorists.'

'Yes?'

'Every time any of these groups run out of cash they pick up the biggest man they can find. Then we do a deal. We never learn.'

'I suppose not,' said Gregory automatically.

When they came through the double glass gates beyond Customs, Gregory immediately focused on the familiar pock-marked face of Mason, the Head of the Institute's London Bureau. Beside him, wearing a chauffeur's uniform that looked two sizes too small, stood a tall, well-built man with short closely cropped hair who Gregory placed at once as one of the heavies from CIA London Station. The liaison man nodded to his colleague and disappeared into the crowd.

'Give me that,' said Mason, reaching for Gregory's case, but before he had time to take it the CIA chauffeur had picked it up with an enormous hand and strode off with it through the deserted reception area. The others followed him outside to where a large glistening black Buick was parked in unique splendour beside the kerb.

'You could hardly have chosen anything more conspicuous,' said Gregory. 'The last shiny car in London? Have it changed.'

'Sure, Max,' said Mason gently. 'CIA trying to make you feel more welcome, that's all.'

The CIA chauffeur set off at high speed along the M4 motorway towards central London. But it began to rain and by the time they reached Chiswick, visibility was bad and he had to slow down to avoid the huge potholes that were all too frequent hazards along the dual carriageway. From the verges, the garbage of years of neglect spilled outwards, adding its own menace. In the distance, the lights that had once illuminated the London skyline glowed only intermittently, and Gregory had to fight back a wave of untypical depression as he sat in silence beside Mason, speculating about where it had all gone wrong.

When they reached the crest of the hill where the M4 hits the rump end of the Cromwell Road, the Buick was forced to a stop at a temporary police barrier that had been created by parking two armoured personnel carriers askew across the roadway. A little beyond, Gregory could make out police in riot gear, while a number of ambulances with wire-mesh over their windows and warning-lights flashing were parked on the opposite carriageway. When he lowered the car window he could hear someone, unseen, haranguing an invisible audience through a megaphone, the words drowned from time to time by shouting and the chanting of unrecognisable slogans.

All at once there was a powerful explosion, and from Earl's Court Road a ball of flame rocketed into the air. From his vantage point in the partial safety of the car, Gregory was given a brief glimpse of something that looked like a body being catapulted through the air and landing, at least part of it, in a shapeless heap not more than fifty yards from where they were. As the noise of the explosion died away, it was replaced by screams and shouts, which the wail of the sirens rose to dominate in their turn. Then renewed, hostile chanting took over again as, from the far side of the road junction, groups of rioters, many dressed in the too-familiar grey denim, appeared from out of the darkness. Waving brickbats and chains, they charged across the road, hell-bent on some unseen foe. The riot police were suddenly nowhere in evidence as, in the distance, the packs engaged, then regrouped. There was a sudden staccato burst of small-arms fire, then the sound of a police megaphone futilely urging people to disperse.

'That's enough of the local colour,' Mason barked at the CIA man. 'Can we move?'

Despite the traffic that had built up around them and with an ability that belied his primal appearance, the driver reacted by pulling the huge Buick round in a sweeping U-turn and, at the expense of a costly dent to the car in front, mounted the soft verge of the motorway. Across a barren building site, the tyres tore the ground and chunks of masonry hit the undercasting, but the driver did not stop till he reached the freedom of a deserted side street.

'Neat,' said Gregory approvingly.

'A few moments longer . . . That was your reintroduction to our incipient civil war,' said Mason slowly. 'One thing we don't do here when that sort of thing is on the boil is stay and watch. Spectators don't last long.'

'I remember,' said Gregory. 'What now?'

'Wait here till things cool. No point in trying to circle round the area on a night like this.'

'How long?'

'Give it half an hour.'

'I'm tired,' said Gregory. 'Sleep is what I need.'

The CIA man killed the lights, got out and shut the door of the car quietly behind him. Through the Buick's smoked-glass windows, Gregory could see him take a gun from a shoulder holster and casually slip it into his jacket pocket.

'You can relax,' said Mason. 'He's good. He'll keep an eye out.'

'Then let's not waste more time. Take me through what you've got laid on.'

'Tell me one thing first,' said Mason. 'About Lou.'

'He's dead. Leave it there.'

Mason failed to grasp Gregory's mood. 'You told me they were the Commander's men. I don't believe it was them though, I really don't. It didn't have the Brother's mark either. So who the . . .?'

'Leave it there, I said.' The vehemence of Gregory's tone bounced Mason into silence.

It took both men some minutes to regain their humour, then Mason produced a rumpled pack of cigarettes as a peace offering. Gregory shook his head. 'You know me better. Tell me about tomorrow.'

'There's not much to tell. I thought I'd wait till you came. I've recruited quite a good little team. Despite the brain drain I've enlisted some bright men; they know the British economy, oil, trade, urban terrorism, the security services . . . you name it.'

'OK.' Gregory cut him short. 'This is what I want. As soon as I've sized your new people up I want you to set up a meeting with the Commander. Then the Brother. Then maybe I'll make a few official calls on the Government.'

'Anything you say, Max.'

'How long will it take you to fix?'

'Like a couple of years.'

'I'm not joking,' said Gregory softly.

'You have to be joking,' said Mason. 'No way are the two hard men going to see you – unless, that is, you have some fantastic excuse you haven't let me in on.'

'I don't have any excuse. But I have my brief.'

'It better be good. You may think that you're a big boy as head of the Institute but that counts for zero here. They don't

69

believe in research or theories, just action. You don't joke around when you're fixing to talk to them. They've picked up a lot of expertise in wasting people who try, and I can think of pleasanter ways to reach the hereafter.'

'Like smoking.'

'I'm not joking either, Max. I sure am not. You pay me a fair sum, but it would have to be tripled before I go into that lion's den.'

'You heard. Start with the Commander. Get a message to him,' said Gregory. 'Tell him you've got a man in from New York who wants to talk to him. Hint but don't say outright that I'm here representing a group in the States which may sympathise with him.'

'Who?'

'Tell him, say, that some branch of the John Birch Society might want to send him funds, weapons, what the hell you like. Just get me an interview.'

'You must be slipping off your chunk.'

'Tell me a better way?'

'The better way is not to begin. It may seem like the Commander runs a bunch of street-corner bully boys, but he's got an intelligence unit and a military arm, with a lot of ex-soldiers and the like, that's pulled together a bag of experience in recent months. He's got his own lines out to America . . . and the Continent, especially Spain and Germany. He knows his sympathisers. He'll smell a rat, even if, by any remote chance, your reputation hasn't gone before you.'

'OK. Drop that line altogether. Tell him the truth. I want to talk to him.'

'Speaking for whom?'

'The President of the United States.'

'I tell him that?' Mason looked at Gregory incredulously.

'Will that make him listen?'

'We could try. Now . . . let's see if we can get out of this damn place.'

Two days later, on Thursday, March 3, shortly after four in

the afternoon, Gregory entered an elegant town house in a little street off Park Lane. To prepare himself, he had re-read the CIA file note on the man he was attempting to meet:

Commander: title adopted by William Joseph Henderson, fifty-nine, leader of the United Action Movement (UAM). Born Manchester, son of Scottish fundamentalist pastor and Yorkshire mother; precise date of birth uncertain. Educated: Manchester Grammar; Services: Royal Navy, transferred Marines 1950–56 for special service in Cyprus on unspecified anti-EOKA duties. MC. Mentioned in despatches. Court Martialled for causing grievous bodily harm to a junior officer and dismissed the Service. Use of title Commander is therefore illegal. Political career: member Conservative Monday Club; forced to resign in late sixties because of extreme views. Local then national organiser National Front. Founder member UAM which was formed from several extreme neo-Nazi and right-wing anti-immigrant and anti-communist movements. A gifted speaker, lay preacher and street activist, he inspires considerable loyalty among his closest followers, a loyalty also maintained by strong physical 'disciplining' of those found guilty of betraying the UAM's policies and objectives . . . (See file PF/936/7 for further background reports and personality assessments.)

The CIA bodyguard, right hand thrust deep in the bulging pocket of his overcoat, followed Gregory unhappily into the hallway, while Mason, who had driven with them, waited where he was in the back of the car outside. The CIA man fumed as two men in paramil uniforms appeared and searched them both, politely and efficiently removing the bodyguard's gun, then showed Gregory alone into a book-lined study where a tall thin man with a well-trimmed moustache stood waiting in front of a roaring fire. It was an almost perfect scene, right down to the expensive crystal decanters on a silver tray and a foxhound asleep on the rug. Only the sub-machine gun and the box of grenades on a side table took the edge off the charm.

The man introduced himself as Colonel Makepeace. 'The Commander is sorry he couldn't see you, Professor Gregory. He's a busy man though he always tries to find time for our American friends. I'm his Head of Information. You'll have to make do with me.'

'Very grateful,' said Gregory carefully. 'An attractive house, you have.'

'Thank you. We believe in keeping certain standards.'

'Not much evidence of gracious living around at the moment.'

'Sadly not. But we will ensure that it will come again. Now: you wanted?'

'I have been asked to come to see you . . .'

'We've dealt with the CIA before.'

'I'm not CIA.'

'Your friend outside is.'

'You're well informed.'

'One of our areas of expertise. In the sort of situation we find ourselves, near-war Professor Gregory, it's essential to be one step ahead. But right now I'm at a slight loss. I'll be frank: I had understood from our intelligence sources that you were working for the CIA . . .'

'I was . . . I still am, or at least my Institute is at research project level. But I personally am here on a new, wider assignment. I've been appointed by the President of the United States as his special envoy to see if there is any way the US Administration can help, can use its good offices in assisting Britain find some solution to its problems.'

The Colonel's response to Gregory's frankness was dry to the point of acidity. 'The American Ambassador and his well-staffed US Embassy in Grosvenor Square?'

'Our experience in the Middle East, and, you may remember, in London itself during the Second World War, has been that the appointment of someone with a single function, that of liaison at the highest personal level . . .'

'I suppose we can't blame the President. The reputation of your present Ambassador to the Court of St James's is on a par with . . . er . . . some of his less distinguished predecessors.'

Gregory avoided being drawn into agreeing. 'I'm not here to undercut the Ambassador or his staff but I am here to listen and to help where I can. I came to you first.'

'I understood so. Very well, Professor,' said the Colonel, cutting the dialogue dead. 'If you want our views, I'll give them to you, whatever your functions really are.' He made a gesture with his right arm towards a leather chair by the fireside, and Gregory, after a moment's delay negotiating his way round the foxhound on the hearth-rug, sank into it.

Gregory watched the Colonel intently. The latter gave no further appearance of interest in Gregory's credentials, or so it seemed, but whatever else he had been well chosen for his role as spokesman. For the next half hour Gregory sat and listened to a glib but increasingly rabid outpouring of policy mixed with prejudice. The Colonel began by praising the 'right-thinking people of Britain' who had been driven to take to the streets in defence of liberty, in defence of the British way of life, in defence of white, ethnic purity. The left had asked for it by their use of undemocratic means in their attempts to usher in moral, political and above all racial decadence. The country had been dragged down by the mismanagement of so-called libertarians and wet-minded liberals. The rot had gone on too long. At last Britain, or some Britons under the Commander, who was a gifted and far-sighted patriot, had come to their senses. They had not wanted to form vigilante groups nor take to the streets, for they believed in the democratic process. But their hands had been forced by the Communists, the blacks, the Pakistanis. The Colonel paused and waved an arm theatrically, in a gesture that threw Gregory back to films he had seen of Germany in the thirties.

'How much have you really achieved, Colonel?' Gregory asked.

'Not much yet, Professor Gregory, but we are winning. We will not rest till we have wiped the Communist scum out of

British politics. We want to make Britain a decent place to live, for decent people. We have, as you doubtless know, a policy, a financially generous scheme for repatriating all blacks . . .'

'You seem to have got rid of the Arabs from central London.' Gregory did not smile.

'I suppose you are right,' the Colonel said. 'That is one good thing. But we still have the enemy within. The so-called Brother, who takes his orders from Moscow, is trying to sap the moral fibre of this country.'

'You think Moscow is behind it all?'

'Who else? At times, admittedly, we are sure they push the Brother further than even he wants to go. Once or twice we've tried to have a ceasefire. He's appeared to go along with it, then . . . it all falls apart again. Of course the Kremlin's behind it. They are the only ones to gain. And they will unless we retain our present highly defensive position.'

'Don't you fear taking Britain over the brink?'

'What brink? The nearest thing to a brink was when we were blind and shackled, when we still allowed the left wing a free rein, and allowed the trade unions and Trotskyites to have their own way. Then we were at the brink. Now we are fighting away from the edge. We, the Commander and all of us in the UAM are determined to ensure that, in the end, Britain will return to being decent, honourable, upright, racially pure.'

There was a long pause, then the Colonel changed tack. 'Over to you, Professor Gregory,' he said.

'As I said, I have been sent to establish contact . . .'

'I heard you. But to what real purpose?'

'The President is very concerned at the way things are going.'

'That raises a lot of questions. Like US interests being at stake?'

'One of the things I would like to talk to the Commander about.'

'I will see what can be arranged. Now that we are sure you

are not here on your own account. We had thought that maybe your brother's murder . . .'

'That has nothing to do with my being here,' said Gregory softly. He stood up.

'Of course not.' The Colonel smiled drily, shook Gregory's hand firmly, and showed him out into the hallway where his bodyguard stood waiting.

In the study, the Colonel picked up a telephone hand-set, pressed a buzzer and waited. Then he spoke: 'Yes, Sir. Him all right . . . From the President personally, he says. We could arrange a meeting, on your terms, Sir, of course.'

In the street, Gregory joined Mason in the back of the battered Humber that had replaced the Buick. The CIA man dominated the driver's seat, seeming even more vast in the smaller British car.

'How did it go?' asked Mason, looking across expectantly.

'I got the front man.'

'As expected,' said Mason. 'By the way, a message for you came on the CIA net while you were in there. Prime Minister Hunt has heard you are here. He wants to see you. He's reported to be very angry that you didn't check in with him first.'

'I'm not good at apologising,' said Gregory.

Nine

THE PRIME MINISTER agreed to see Gregory at twenty-one hundred hours that same evening. Coming direct from what Mason cynically called a wounded pride meeting with the highly antagonistic US Ambassador at the Grosvenor Square Embassy, Gregory was twenty minutes late as a result of the series of security checks he had to submit himself to before he reached Downing Street. He met the first roadblock by the Whitehall Theatre, once the home of topless farce; the second was sited opposite the Horse Guards where, long since, the ceremonial guard had dismounted for the last time; while at the end of Downing Street itself, Gregory had to leave Mason and his bodyguard in the car and, after a meticulous body search, be escorted the rest of the way on foot. Pausing at the door of Number Ten, he glanced round briefly. Long gone were the tourists with their cameras; gone too was the curious normality that had once pervaded this unimpressive little London back street. In its place there were tangles of barbed wire and anti-bomb mesh, with arc-lights and remote-control TV cameras constantly searching everywhere. The police on duty at the barriers wore steel helmets and carried sub-machine guns; there was one army detachment permanently sited in an armoured scout-car at the Whitehall end of the street while another was strategically placed by the railings opposite the door of Number Eleven Downing Street. Opposite, on the roof of the Foreign Office, unsightly watch-towers had become a permanent feature atop the building. As a sad little genuflection to normality, the two British bobbies outside the door to Number Ten itself still wore their traditional blue uniforms and helmets, and one even managed a friendly salute as he opened the door for Gregory. Inside the hall, a uniformed guard accosted him and, after walking him through a metal detector frame, subjected him to a further body search. 'Sorry about that, Sir,' said the man, pleasantly.

A dapper Private Secretary in a pinstripe suit appeared from nowhere. 'Professor Gregory? So glad you could come at such short notice. No . . . Don't worry about being a bit late, Sir. The Prime Minister's quite used to it. He's waiting for you now. Do come this way.' The accent was impeccably bland and Oxbridge.

He was led up a dimly lit flight of stairs and past the long line of portraits of previous prime ministers which included, near the end of the row, that of the only woman who for a term had held that high office. Number Ten, along with most Government offices, functioned on its own emergency generators, and, as he went, Gregory noted their background hum as he did the steel riot doors, new since his last visit more than seven years earlier. Halfway up the stairs, he stood to one side to allow a woman to pass. Her face, half in shadow, seemed to smile at him. There was something about her and the way she moved, and instinctively he turned to watch her go. But she turned a corner and vanished like a shadow and he was left wondering if the poor light had played tricks with his memory.

He was shown into the Prime Minister's study. Harold Hunt, shorter and rather flabbier than his photographs suggested, stood up behind his desk, hand outstretched. 'Glad you could fit me in, Professor.' The Prime Minister looked grim and his voice was irritable and brisk.

'I didn't expect you to know I was here, Prime Minister,' said Gregory, with a touch of an apology.

'Friends in high places,' said the Prime Minister. 'Your President rang. Should I say the American President? D'you still keep your British passport?'

'Yes . . . I, well . . .' Gregory hadn't expected such immediate hostility, just as he could have done with some warning that the President was going to cart him by telling Hunt of his mission so soon. He suspected that the Ambassador must have put the White House up to it and made a mental note to watch that particular line-up for the future.

'I didn't need him to tell me, of course. We may appear to be in a bit of chaos but I'm glad to say our intelligence services are still working well. A report came through twenty-four hours ago, reporting your arrival the other night, and we were doing our own trace when the President's call came, explaining why you're here. A useful thought, though it would have been kind to give advance notice. I will not be bullied, Professor. Not by anyone, even our friends. I'm also informed that the CIA have got you a clean bill of health from the Metropolitan Police . . . that unfortunate matter after your brother's death. I'll be blunt: it would never have got past me if I'd known, self-defence or not. Anyway, it's done. And between you and me, I'm not too upset. Also . . . well, your being here may just be useful. Give a little depth to a relationship that's been going a bit stale and empty. Afraid I don't have too much time for your Ambassador, you see. Never was one for political appointees. They don't have the depth of experience of professional diplomats, don't you think?'

The querulous and jumpy tenor of Hunt's remarks put Gregory additionally on his guard. 'It's kind of you to see me, Mr Prime Minister,' he said cautiously. 'I was going to ask to see you, but first I wanted to brief myself more fully on what is going on.'

'The Commander . . . so-called?'

'I haven't seen him.'

'Not for want of trying, I believe.'

'I didn't want to waste your time.'

'You don't spend much of your life doing that, Professor. The Gregory Institute spends a lot of effort and money working on the British problem. The "British predicament", I think you call it. It is nice to be thought of as a predicament – just one more international crisis. It must be reassuring to be able to sit high up in your office, in Madison Avenue isn't it?, thinking about poor old Britain as a problem like Cuba, the Panama Canal, Vietnam, Iran or Poland.' The Prime Minister paused and stared intently at Gregory.

'Yes, Prime Minister,' came the subdued response.

'If you're really here to help, Gregory, don't start by playing games. The US press have me labelled as one of the weakest prime ministers this century, but I didn't get where I am without knowing how to judge people. If your President wants to help with the "British predicament", that's fine. But keep it clean. If you're his personal emissary, I'll talk to you, but only as long as you are honest with me, Professor. All above board. If you're talking to the Commander or the Communists or anyone else, I want to know. This is my country, d'you understand? I still have some power. And some self-respect.'

'Prime Minister, I don't know what you have heard but . . .'

'Don't give me that, Professor Gregory. I'll give you only one chance.'

'I'm not sure what you're driving at . . . The President asked me, with my British background and the expertise of my Institute, to come here with an offer of assistance, advice if you like. I don't know what kind of advice that will eventually be, or whether you'll want to take it. I haven't had sufficient time to study the problem on the ground. Of course I have all the reports: my Institute, the State Department and the CIA have all been working hard on Britain.'

'I bet you have.'

'Prime Minister, if this is going to work out we have, as you said, to start by being honest. Your phrase. Unless you believe in what I'm here for, there's little point my going on.'

'Agreed.'

'Then?'

'Then let me ask about American motives, since that's what international politics is all about.'

'The US Government has a massive interest in the Western Alliance and the maintenance of the European balance of power. It is one of the highest priorities of United States policy to ensure that Britain doesn't come apart at the seams.'

'Great stuff . . . for a first-year course in politics,' interrupted the Prime Minister. 'But why?'

'I've just explained. The balance of power . . . A weak Britain means a weak NATO.'

'Balls, Gregory. Spheroids . . . Crap. That's not the real nitty-gritty of why you're here. I know that and if you don't realise it then you're a fool.'

There was a pause. 'You tell me, Prime Minister.'

'I know the only reason you, Auerbach and Admiral what's-his-name are worried and why you've put your shadow of a President up to this little scheme.'

'Yes?'

'You're not interested in whether this particular British Government survives. But you do want to be about when whatever happens happens and then you'll be ready to stand and be counted as loyal friends of the new régime, the first in on the act with fistfuls of dollars at the ready. International diplomacy's answer to the Vicar of Bray.'

'With respect, Prime Minister . . .'

'Don't "with respect" me, Professor. When my civil servants come to me with that jargon it puts me on my highest guard. Now . . . where was I? Yes, I know that in the American book almost any British Government is as good as the next, though a good tough right-wing one would suit you best . . .'

'Because I'm trying to get to talk to the Commander doesn't mean . . .'

'No, of course it doesn't. All sweetness and light and just trying to find out what fascism is about, aren't you Professor, to help you understand our predicament?'

'I tell you, I'm here to act as the President's personal link with you.'

'With me until I don't exist, Professor. Then the next man, the next prime minister. And if it's the Commander, well, the Americans are good at handling fascist dictators, except that the Gregory Institute would be set the task of finding a new, respectable word to replace fascism and then get down to telling the world what a good bunch of guys Britain's latter-day Hitlers are. That so?'

'Sir. I protest . . .'

'Protest away. The US Government has one and only one role over here and that's to keep the Kremlin out. Anyone who's capable of doing that, be it H. Hunt Esquire or his heirs and successors, is fine by you boys. And as far as Moscow is concerned it's a *vice versa* situation, except that in their case they don't like any of the alternative candidates for power including the so-called Brother's mob, who, if I'm to believe my intelligence people, are considered too indisciplined and uncooperative to take any sort of line from Moscow.'

'So what conclusion do you draw, Prime Minister?'

'That the Russians will go to any lengths to avoid a settlement being reached until they have achieved the right degree of chaos and the right candidates to run a real revolution over here.'

'Anything we can do . . .'

'Generous as always, the Americans. But it needs more than you to solve our problems.' The Prime Minister stopped for a moment and when he started talking again he was a shade less hostile. 'We almost seemed to be getting there on our own. We got a long way with both factions round the negotiating table. Midnight sessions, beer and sandwiches and even touches of old-fashioned, good-natured humour. Then . . . bang. The end of hope came spewing out of the barrels of anonymous guns.'

'The Russians?'

'Who else? At one time I thought that they . . . From telephone surveillance, bugs at the Brother's HQ, we knew that even they think their Moscow comrades are behind it. That makes the Brother think and think hard about his Communist allies. That's why I felt there was some real hope of getting him on board. But then came the killing and we had each side blaming the other again.'

'Can't you give them proof of what the Russians are doing?'

'I'm working on that now. People may think I'm a wet.

Well, Professor Gregory, they don't know Harold Hunt. And I have another card up my sleeve . . .'

'Sir?'

'Oil, of course. North Sea oil. British oil.'

'Important factor, Prime Minister. But not over-riding, since it only provides a tiny fraction of total world resources. You'll know I've been working on a project . . .'

'Exactly. So you know all about the Unst Field and the blocks around it?'

'That's part of the Norslag Concession. Low grade stuff. Difficult to extract . . .'

A desk telephone gave an urgent bleep. As the Prime Minister moved to pick it up he turned and said: 'D'you know, Gregory, maybe it's not that you're a fool, you just don't know . . .' He paused. 'Hello? Yes, what is it? I said I was not to be disturbed.' Hunt's voice was powerful and, for a brief instant, Gregory had a glimpse of the hidden determination in him. But a moment later that judgement fell away as the Prime Minister seemed to crumple, his face went white and he leaned forward on the desk for support. Then, after a few seconds' pause, he fell back into his chair, still clutching the receiver, so that, as he moved, the telephone itself was pulled off the desk with a crash.

'What . . .? Where . . .?' the Prime Minister was muttering. 'What did you say? No, I cannot . . . Yes. Yes, come in, damn you.'

'Prime Minister?' Gregory rose from his chair and came forward while the other man sat slumped where he was, still holding the receiver and staring into space. Two of Hunt's officials burst into the room. One of them went up to him while the other pulled Gregory aside and whispered urgently in his ear.

'You'll have to go now, Professor. It's his granddaughter. Kidnapped from her parents' flat about twenty minutes ago. Her bodyguard's shot up . . . God . . . They even bring children into the war . . .'

'I'll leave you,' said Gregory, moving to the door. 'Prime Minister, may I . . .'

'No, no,' the Prime Minister suddenly sat up. 'Let the man stay. If he wants to know what's going on here, this'll give him . . . he'll see what a sick society we have. Oh Christ, my son . . . what he'll be going through.'

Despite his own cold, unemotional style, Gregory was alive to the fact that other people had very different ways of reacting to crises in their personal lives. He had seen world leaders and captains of industry take far-reaching and heartless decisions that affected the well-being of countless others in their professional lives, and had watched the same people fall apart when it came to domestic issues. It was not to be so with the Prime Minister who, with a supreme effort, galvanised himself into action, stood up and started bellowing orders at the two private secretaries, at an Assistant Commissioner of Police who had appeared in the doorway and at numerous unnamed people at the receiving end of his loudspeaker telephone. Gregory sat, watched and took dispassionate note of how Hunt, despite the emotional strain he was under, was successfully getting the whole security apparatus put on full alert.

Two hours later he was still there, having learned much about the workings of the British state and more about its Prime Minister. A bottle of whisky had been produced and in the last hour over half of it had been drunk, Hunt and Gregory keeping glass for glass with each other. During that time and in between phone calls and security briefings, Hunt gradually dropped his hectoring tone and began to talk in more human terms about what he had done and was still trying to do to bring reason to British politics. He appeared to hold little back in describing the long yet fruitful negotiations which had been chaired by his former Minister of Defence and which eventually led to the leaders of both sides agreeing to a secret meeting on HMS *Bulwark*, the Royal Naval frigate moored for the occasion in the Pool of London. Hunt told Gregory, as he had Lateman of AP, how he himself had taken the chair on that occasion and, after an all-night session, had managed to get the

Commander and the Brother to agree to call a truce and to attend a more formal meeting of conciliation at Lancaster House. Hunt had left the ship in the early hours of that morning believing that he had achieved something and convinced in his own mind that both leaders shared his view that nothing was to be gained by continuing with the present strife. A matter of hours later, the assassination first of the Defence Minister and then of the Commander's ADC was followed by an upsurge in street violence and a total breakdown of the brief trust which had been built up at the conference table.

Gregory tried to question Hunt. 'What d'you think the Russians will do next?' he asked gently.

Hunt shook his head wearily. At that moment a telephone call came through, Hunt jumped up to seize it and the answer to Gregory's question was lost. It was one more negative report: from the kidnappers there was silence; no ransom demands, no threats. Around one in the morning Gregory stood up and tried to leave but as he did so one of the Prime Minister's private secretaries came in with news that the body of a young girl had been found in a shallow grave close to the M1 motorway about fifty miles north of London. Immediately on its heels came a further message: tests had proved that the body was that of an older child.

'I'm relieved for you, Prime Minister,' Gregory said softly.

'Relieved? Are you relieved? About the child's body? Yes . . . I'm sorry. I don't mean it. Now it's some other parent or grandparent who has the tragedy.'

Nothing more was said; and then: 'If you'll excuse me Professor – Max. Max . . . I'll call you Max. I must get some sleep now.'

'Yes, Prime Minister. Good night, Prime Minister. Thank you for your time.'

Gregory left Hunt alone. Outside the study door the man in the pinstripe suit, now less dapper and grey with fatigue, was waiting to show him the front door. Despite the lateness of the hour the staff offices beyond were full of people and activity and Gregory glimpsed, through one open door, a desk at which a woman sat, her back towards him. He hesitated, as if to move forward into the room, but the pinstriped man showed him firmly out into the night.

Mason was moaning. 'A hell of a time. Why the devil did you wait so long? I heard about his grandchild. Poor bugger . . .'

'I'll explain tomorrow,' Gregory muttered.

'I can't wait,' said Mason.

'You've been to Number Ten quite a bit?' Gregory asked, as they drove away. He concentrated to keep the question casual and the slur of the whisky out of his voice.

'Half a dozen times over the years.'

'Know the staff?'

'Some of them.'

'There's a girl, she's got . . .'

'For God's sake, Max,' said Mason. 'You're drunk, you lucky sod.'

Ten

THE DAY that followed was another active one for Dan Lateman. By early evening he had already put two substantial stories and a background brief on the wires and the night was still young.

AP, London, Friday, March 4. Dan Lateman reporting: Special Presidential Envoy.

'Spokesperson at Ten Downing Street, traditional town-house residence of British Prime Minister, refused to confirm tonight that US President has sent Professor Max Gregory, currently head of prestigious, New York-based Gregory Institute, as his personal envoy to Premier Hunt. Informed sources claim this as last ditch attempt by US Administration to assist centrist British Government's efforts to return the riot-torn country to law and democracy. The presence in tense, bomb-scarred London tonight of British-born Gregory, has, repeat has, been confirmed by London Institute's bureau chief, Sandy Mason, who described the Professor's visit as strictly routine. High-placed Whitehall sources have indicated, however, that at a secret unscheduled meeting with Premier Hunt last evening, Gregory brought message of support from the President for the Premier's efforts to achieve a peaceful settlement of rightist-Marxist street conflicts. Reports also indicate strong US backing for all measures directed at maintenance of UK position in NATO and other Western defence arrangements, inclusive of retaining US military bases on the British mainland. UK Government sources have also indicated concern at reports that US Administration and CIA, under direction of ex-navy hero Admiral Cassover, have been exercised by evidence of increased Soviet involvement in UK internal affairs. Indication is that Soviets have indeed been active in support of leftist leaders, including so-called Brother, repeat Brother, and also, independently, have fomented crisis by use of ultra-left, action terrorist squad. Group is identical to that accused of car-bomb murder of English, correction, British, Defence Minister at crucial stage in secret left-rightist negotiations on board British naval ship last month. *More to follow.*'

AP, London, Friday, March 4. Dan Lateman reporting: Kidnapping.

'British press have now lifted self-imposed ten-hour black-out on news that Premier Hunt's granddaughter, Elizabeth Jane, ten, repeat ten, has been kidnapped from her Kensington Gardens, London apartment. Girl's bodyguard, Maurice McNally, thirty-three, unmarried, was fatally injured by one of three masked gunmen who broke into girl's apartment while parents were attending local vigilante-run personal defence course. So far understood that there have been no, repeat no, ransom demands or other contact with kidnappers. Rightist and left-wing groups have so far disclaimed all responsibility for kidnapping. *Ends.*'

AP, London, Friday, March 4. Background brief by Dan Lateman: Vigilantes.

'Formation of vigilantes, or "street troopers" as they are commonly known, on an organised basis, was an inevitable reaction to the escalation of street violence in urban Britain. First formed in the early eighties, mainly in decaying inner-city areas, they were to act as a counter-measure to mob hooliganism and racial unrest. Where law enforcement agencies were under strain and short of manpower and with military support needed elsewhere, the civil authorities tended to turn a blind eye when vigilantes increasingly took the law into their own hands, arguably to protect lives and property. For some time these groups had a generally calming effect, but naturally appealing more to right-wing elements they were gradually subsumed by the Commander's units. Leftists reacted rapidly by forming their own platoons of "people's militia" to police areas in which they had high levels of support. Gradually para-military uniforms were adopted by both sides, and while all groups still claim to be unarmed it is common knowledge that one qualification for membership is access to a rifle or handgun. Currently, only in suburban and rural areas do real "community vigilante" groups operate. Few villages are now without trained units of citizens who provide local "border guards", patrols and control posts. Legitimate law enforcement authorities have accepted the situation since it is one over which they cannot hope to have any control. *Ends.*'

At ten thirty-five that same evening, Friday, March 4, the CIA's prime mole at the Embassy of the USSR in Kensington Palace Gardens, London, Bucur Popov, passed on the latest batch of photo-copied, top-secret Russian reports to his American controller. The content of one of these clearly indicated the Russian Ambassador's puzzlement at the degree to which the Soviet Union was being blamed for fomenting the current civil unrest in Britain.

The Soviet Government and people [the Ambassador, as always, chose his words carefully] have long been accused by capitalists and neo-fascist governments and their running-dogs of attempting to promote revolution in many parts of the world. Whatever the justification for such accusations elsewhere and in the past, as the Politbureau knows and has agreed, activities on this score in Britain have been very limited indeed and have been confined to certain financial and propaganda backing for legitimate Marxist-Communist cells. While lies are to be expected from the right wing and from the weak centrist Government in order to excuse the mistakes of its current policies, it is of considerable concern that several factions of the left, including the PSC Executive, led by Comrade Paul Verity, have privately expressed the view that the Soviet Union and its agencies have been responsible for promoting active unrest, financing assassination squads and other illegitimate activities. Despite the seriousness of these accusations, I recommend that there should be no, repeat no, public response to such accusations until further information from intelligence sources has been elicited as to why they are being made against the Soviet Government at this juncture and who might hope to gain from blackening the good name of the heroic Soviet Peoples.

This was one of very few secret reports on the UK political scene that the CIA did not pass to the Gregory Institute in New York or to the President's special envoy in London.

Five p.m., New York time, on this day of apparently unconnected events, and in the Ops Room of the Gregory Institute in New York, oil economist Mick Vanderman, in common with the less dedicated of his colleagues, was working with some of the pressure off. There was always the same temptation when Professor Gregory was abroad, and Vanderman had taken the opportunity to have a rather lengthy lunch with an old MIT colleague at P. J. Clark's, and had returned to the Institute in a mood of general well-being and contentment. Tonight he would be able to get away in time for a shower and change of shirt before taking his somewhat impetuous girlfriend to see the new Broadway show, to which that morning's *Times* had given an intelligently welcoming review.

Vanderman had not set out to have an idle afternoon for he was conscientious if not outstanding at his job; he enjoyed the work and was pleased to have been selected personally by Gregory to work on the British project. He was of course well qualified for the task, not least because of his year at the Oil

Technology Department at Heriot-Watt College in Edinburgh finalising his Ph.D. thesis, which had provided him with first-hand experience of the British contribution. But he felt himself less than competent and somewhat muddle-headed as a result of his heavy lunch, when the figures he had left to be programmed reappeared on his desk. For the second time in two days the computer had turned out a nonsense – absurd estimates for potentially recoverable North Sea resources. So, painstakingly, Vanderman set out to check sources, double-verify Government and oil company predictions and cross-relate to known reserves. Then he put them through the computer link with the CIA, but no way did they match. Conclusion: either he or the computer was at fault, or someone was pushing out a false bundle of statistics, a massively false bundle.

In the end he put the tables and the print-out aside, picked up *Business Week* magazine and put it in his briefcase. He looked at his watch and stood up. It was too late on a Friday evening; he would come back and track down his error in the clear light of a new week.

Eleven

AT THE expense of two or three minor infringements of the truth, Gregory extracted from an unsuspecting CIA Head of Station some of the information he required. She was one of Whitehall's brightest: secretary of an important Cabinet Committee, well-trusted by the Prime Minister, unmarried as far as anyone knew, eleven years older but the same Eileen Byrne.

With uncharacteristic apprehension he telephoned her at Number Ten and announced himself. There was an over-long pause, then: 'I half-expected you to call . . . No, I didn't realise it was you; not until afterwards. That you'd arrived here was only known to a handful of people.' Her voice was distant rather than hostile, so he followed through and asked politely if they might meet.

'I suppose so,' she said. He could discern no emotion whatsoever in her reply.

Some of the fashionably picturesque features of Langan's Brasserie in Stratton Street, the eclectic selection of paintings and the white-aproned waiters, remained, though its former liveliness of character had been largely extinguished by the security guards at the doors, the wire mesh and steel shutters over the windows and the sparseness of the custom. But somehow or other, despite the shortages, the lack of fresh meat and vegetables, Mason had told him that they still managed to maintain a reasonable standard of cuisine.

The evening started out badly and went on that way for quite some time. Gregory began it by having a row with CIA Head of Station over wanting to stand his bodyguard down for the night, but in the end he got his way. When he met Eileen Byrne as arranged at the restaurant, the going was cold verging on icy. He had become used to handling bright American girls and considered that he knew where to begin and where to end a relationship. In a decade he felt he had never failed to pigeonhole a new protagonist by type, and once in that pigeonhole the rest was easy. But Eileen Byrne fitted not at all and his memories of a naive twenty-three-year-old died an immediate death. He found himself faced with a hard but not yet hard-bitten adversary; every time he thought he had her summed up, she changed tack and left him stumbling. Intelligent, yes; an assistant secretary for economic policy at Number Ten was, by definition, not likely to be a dunce. Attractive – she had obviously matured well and now knew how to handle her advantage.

But the evening was not just his one-sided and increasingly unhappy attempt at a nostalgia trip; she too, though she hid it better, was curious about this acceptedly brilliant and powerful man who had suddenly reappeared in her life. Her memories of him were less vivid than his of her and she concentrated on the present, a rich, harshly good-looking but obvious mark-one bastard. She had one major advantage over him which she would use: she had seen the British Intelligence file on him and knew a lot about his recent successes, his few failures and all about Lou.

For the first half hour they exchanged platitudes, then: 'You remember New York?' he asked eventually.

'It was an event in my life. You were.' She shrugged uninterested.

'It was going so well.'

'Was it? For you perhaps.'

'Then you disappeared. No warning.'

'It was the only way. I wasn't strong enough to handle it otherwise. Then.'

'And?'

'And I went back to England and decided to take the Civil Service entrance exams. Maybe you don't remember . . . what

92

flipped me . . .' She paused. 'You sent your chauffeur and car to pick me up – bring me back to your flat to be waiting when you decided to turn up.'

'I did?'

'You did.'

'Bitter?'

'I suppose so.'

'It took me a while to realise . . .' he began, looking straight at her.

'You want me to believe that sort of line?' she asked, looking back at him, unblinking.

In different circumstances she might have decided to succumb once again when he switched into a dominating overture, but that was not the way she wanted the game this time. As a result they took an hour or so pacing each other uneasily over the escargots and the lamb in rosemary, with her defensive, then belligerent, he hostile, then arrogant. They were both pitching for an early night and each going their separate way.

The thaw came as the result of an outside diversion. A large, roseate fellow-diner at a neighbouring table, a man with a loud voice and demanding habits, had, for unexplained but understandable reasons, a large plate of cream-topped trifle emptied over him by the fat, blowsy blonde who sat with him. Both stormed out in dramatic rage leaving much laughter behind them and the Byrne–Gregory dinner was saved. Their common mirth was helped by another bottle of house red in breaking down the barriers, and their eyes met properly across the table for the first time.

'Death to memories,' he said raising his glass in a mock toast.

'Why not,' she replied, with the beginnings of a smile.

It was ten p.m. London time and five hours behind that in New York where Mick Vanderman, with much less experience than his boss, was also having advanced girlfriend trouble. The problem with this particular girl was that she had ideas above his station with regard to bachelor Vanderman's status and, more importantly, his salary. The lady had ambitions for them both which did not include marrying someone with a grey, nine-to-five job behind some computer at the Gregory Institute. Her requirements were for a bright young executive who would give her a modern house somewhere in a fashionable part of Long Island and a couple of equally fashionable small children to go with it. She wanted an advance on what they both had had in their Brooklyn upbringing, and Mick Vanderman was going through a bout of feeling inadequate in the realisation that he was not living up to her expectations.

Vanderman knew only too well that he should be sorting out the complex nonsense he had made over the British oil statistics, but the clear head required for that task was constantly being waylaid by thoughts of her. He had got into the habit of calling her frequently to ensure that she was content, and a considerable amount of the rest of the time he spent pre-packaging their time together. Tickets to Broadway shows that were too expensive, roses, boxes of chocolates well beyond his day-to-day means, and still she had showed a lack of appreciation. With all that in the forefront of his life, it was easy to put the work of the Institute and especially the need to reprogramme boring figures of oil reserves very low down on his list of priorities. Had it not blown into a flaming row the previous night with her threatening to date an old boyfriend, and his consequent decision to break it off, at least for the next few hours, there would have been an important gap in the historical progression. Late that same evening he had abandoned her in fury and picked up a cab to take him back to the Madison Avenue headquarters of the Gregory Institute.

On the fortieth floor there was still a skeleton staff working on major projects, since, with computers as costly as these, Gregory himself had insisted on a twenty-four-hour usage programme. Nobody paid much attention when Vanderman walked in and over to his desk where, in a ferment of self-righteous indignation building up to remorse, he started working through the oil statistics in an attempt to drive the girl from his mind. He began by cross-checking the projected totals for the various North Sea fields, including the Brent and Forties blocks, which had failed to tally earlier. Then he played them through again on his desk computer terminal, checking sources and making one or two matrix runs against estimates which one of his colleagues had worked out on the fringes of a Middle East oil project. Finally, in an old-fashioned way, he took up a pencil and a pad of lined paper. By the end of all this, at three in the morning, he had forgotten his girl crisis and had proved to himself that either someone somewhere was fixing the figures or that there was the most monstrous error in the projected Unst Field totals. Maximum known reserves in British waters, the absolute maximum, was something in the region of seventy-five billion barrels. The figures which stared up at him from his pad showed a projected estimate several times in excess of those for that field alone. Additionally, the Norslag Corporation, the biggest operator in the area since their take-over, not only of BP, but also of British National Oil Corporation interests and much of Burmah Oil, were showing planned investment figures for their huge Unst concession which could only be justified if the expected yield was believed to be several times published estimates. Norslag, with their tax-loophole headquarters in Paris and Oslo and their reputed under-the-counter deals with the Soviet Union, were the sharpest of operators, particularly with regard to investment planning and research. It was bloody absurd. No way could that block of sea hide such amounts of oil or justify their budgeting.

Around four in the morning he staggered to a couch in the Institute canteen and tried to sleep. After a miserable few hours, half-dozing and worrying more about girlfriend than oil, he returned to the office in a bedraggled state of mind. In the middle of that confused morning he made two or three attempts to ring her to see if he could patch things up but there was no reply. In search of a palliative he went from office to office seeking out the more sympathetic of his colleagues to try out on them the oil figures but they were all distinctly unimpressed, and with the scale of apparent error, were, in their various ways, dismissive. 'You've made some howling mistake, Kid. Go back to school. Work through it again.' 'If you can believe that, fellow, you can believe anything. Go have a shave and shower: that'll wake you up.' 'Look, boy, why don't we talk about it some time when I've got an hour or two and you've gotten a bunch more work done on the project.'

Vanderman brooded for several hours, pulled through some more checks, failed to make contact with his girlfriend a couple more times, then at five p.m. New York time, just about the moment Gregory and Eileen Byrne were leaving Langan's Brasserie, rang Mason in London.

Mason was blunt. 'OK. You're a good boy, Mick, but make it snappy. What's on your mind? I got so many problems here, most of them somebody called Max Gregory, so it better be good.'

'The Unst Field oil figures, Mr Mason, they're all haywire.' He explained his findings, then went on: 'And there's another thing I don't understand. The way I read it, the Norslag Corporation have an investment programme that could no way be justified by known reserves.'

'Norslag have the best man in the business. So that makes you nuts,' said Mason. 'Wait till I tell Max Gregory about you, son. Been sniffing something too strong, have you?'

'Look Mr Mason, I'm serious. I tell you I have multiple-programmed these figures and no way do they gel. You try.'

'This is an open line, Mick. I don't want any eavesdroppers to think we employ sci-fi enthusiasts. You're telling me that Norslag believes there's x-times more oil available in the Unst concession than any of us has known about till now?' Mason's cynicism stretched the Atlantic with abundant clarity.

'I'm only telling you what the figures say. That's what I'm paid to do. I've got figures and I want to check them with CIA at Langley. Can you give me the go-ahead for that, please?'

Mason stood behind his desk in the Institute's London

Bureau, staring at the phone. He did not know whether to be angry or to laugh, as both he and Gregory thought highly of Vanderman.

'OK, OK, boy. Get these figures over here by safe hand, will you. Then we'll decide. Don't wire them, because people are curious. What you can do is . . .'

That was the moment when the door of Mason's office burst inwards and a man with a sten-gun appeared, blazing away from the hip. Mason had no time to look astonished before he was splattered out of view behind his desk. Then from behind the assailant came the sound of further shots and an explosion which knocked him flying and the gun out of his hand. Some time after that Mason remembered that he began, slowly and painfully, to drag himself towards the flame-filled door. From then on everything was blank.

At the Institute, Mick Vanderman stood with the lifeless telephone receiver in his hand, staring at it as if it was responsible for its sudden loss of sound. The series of staccato noises before the line had gone dead could have been interference followed by a break-down, but he sensed something more substantial than that. Stopping a colleague who was going off duty, he tried to share his anxieties but the response was gloomily unimpressive: 'They've had so many strikes in the telecom network over there it's hardly surprising if the lines go down. Or maybe it's another bomb at the exchange. Nothing to worry about, Mick. Mason will be back on line in twenty minutes.'

'You want to go firm on that?'

The other man went without responding and Vanderman was left wondering whether he was making too much, first of the Norslag concession figures, then this. Whatever else, he would now have to wait before cross-checking the figures with CIA, Langley. He stood silent for a moment. Around him was the busy normality of the Gregory Institute; the clicking of the printers, the rattle of tape machines and the distant hum of New York City going home for the night.

Twelve

THEY PAUSED at the corner of Stratton Street and looked across Piccadilly to where the lights of the Ritz still sparkled in an impression of opulent normality.

'As retribution for having stood down my bodyguard they took away my Embassy car and driver. D'you mind walking to the Institute offices? Mason has a car waiting there to take you home. It's only two blocks.'

'Who's Mason?' asked Eileen Byrne.

'Head of my London ops. Salt of the earth and bright even when he's drunk . . . Are we all right walking here?'

'In this part of London? Yes, it's still well policed.'

They were aware of the sound of sirens and shouting even before they turned into Bond Street where the London bureau of the Gregory Institute was housed in an opulent suite of rooms at the top of an eight-storey office block. Or where the bureau had been, for, beyond where the street was blocked by fire engines, they saw at once that the building itself was already a flaming, red-windowed shell. Arc lights played over the scene, picking out and dancing with the jets from the fire hoses. As they stopped in horror, an ambulance tore past them and on into the darkness. There were no onlookers.

Gregory started to move forward, but Eileen put out a restraining hand and grabbed him.

'No. Don't go.'

'Mason's in there.' He turned, white faced, his voice choking.

'Whatever's happened, there's no point in you throwing yourself onto the flames. You realise what'll happen?'

'What will?'

'Appearing at the scene of a crime. Automatically pulled in for questioning. It's always the same.'

'What crime?'

'That fire started by accident?'

'That's my office.'

'They don't know that and they don't care. I warn you, they arrest on sight. We're too close even now. Keep back in the shadows.'

'Mason . . .'

'What can you do that the firemen can't? We'll go to my flat and ring from there. You can get on to the Embassy or I'll ask someone at Number Ten to find out what happened and where this Mason is. No use asking the people on the spot. I promise you.'

'I must, and now. I'm going . . .'

'No. Please. Please, Max.' He again turned to look at her, her expression and her first use of his christian name making him hesitate. 'Where's your flat? Let's go.'

'South Kensington.'

'My hotel's in Park Lane. Much nearer.'

'No, you mustn't go there.'

'Why the hell not? You're acting like a nanny.'

'Believe me.' It was an order more than a plea. She was staring at him, her face lit by the flickering flames from the burning building.

'What the hell d'you mean? You're hiding something. You knew about this, did you?' He swung round at her. 'Did you know . . . Did you know this was going to happen?'

'Of course I didn't know.' She tried to draw away, but he had grabbed her arm and held it tightly. 'There's been a lot of talk about you, that's all. You know that. People don't like you. They've gone to the trouble of killing your brother and now burning your office, so they won't stop at burning you too. Please listen: your hotel's the last place to go right now. Look, we'll have to walk. It's not often . . . that I plead with people to come back with me.'

99

'It's not?' he asked, though it came out worse than he intended.

'You're a bastard, Max Gregory . . . No change.' She turned on her heel and walked away. After a moment's pause he followed her.

In the comfortable setting of her flat he began to regain his composure and look around him. He took in the stimulating paintings on the walls, the deep chairs, the subtle lighting and an academic muddle of books and magazines. Having failed to get any sense from the Embassy, or to raise the CIA Head of Station, he had left it to her and she had now been on the telephone to Number Ten for the past twenty minutes, patiently coaxing information from her harassed colleagues. After a lot of hanging on she was given a partial report on the fire at the Institute: a hundred-pound bomb, plus napalm, and the building was now totally gutted. Only a handful of people had been inside at the time; two men, one a security guard and another suffering from bullet wounds, had been taken by ambulance to the emergency department of Westminster Hospital. There was no information on the identity of the second man or of his condition, nor had anyone claimed responsibility for the attack.

'It has to be Mason.'

'I seem to remember you lecturing people about not jumping to conclusions. I'll try casualties first,' she said coldly, still deeply angry at him for his remark. He watched as she made a number of unsuccessful attempts to get through to the hospital; the line was either engaged or rang on unanswered.

'The surprise is if hospitals answer the phone at all now.' She hesitated. 'I'll try for a duty car to take me there.'

'Why should *you*? It's not your concern; and you don't even know him. I'm going.'

She paused briefly before replying: 'That's another of your bad ideas. If they're looking for you and you're not at your hotel, they'll expect you to go after Mason.'

'Who the hell are "they" you keep talking about?'

'I don't have answers like that. That's your job. If you accept somebody's after you, it's better not to test to see whether I'm correct or not.'

'What have you heard about me?' he asked.

'I told you. Successful, trusted by the President of the United States, a buddy of Admiral Cassover, not best friends with the Secretary of State, and sent here to help us.'

'Like the things wrong with GI's: over-paid, over-sexed and over here.'

She ignored the joke. 'I read the report about your brother and that you had a gun . . .' she paused.

'And?'

'Current assessment: a hard man. I could have told them that. You have a lot of enemies, in particular one bunch with more venom than normal.'

'Why does the Prime Minister think I'm a target?'

'He explained. Our two warring tribes are too interested in getting at each other to bother about transients from your side of the Atlantic. So . . .'

'A third force.'

'A Moscow-backed hit-squad with two roles: keeping things on the boil until the Kremlin is ready and keeping the US in general and you in particular from having any more say.'

'Not a shred of evidence did he offer to back that theory up. He might have told me more but he cut off when he got the news about his granddaughter.'

She shrugged. 'Poor man. He doesn't deserve it. Did he tell you about the meeting on the ship?'

'Yes.'

'I was there. I sat in, taking the record.'

'Why you?'

'He likes me. I tell you, he's not as weak as he's painted, but everything's loaded against him. He had these two men leaving that boat, wanting to agree, realising the futility of violence. All they had to avoid was losing face.'

101

There was a long silence. Eventually Gregory stood up. 'I have to go.'

'For God's sake then get that bodyguard of yours to go with you . . .'

The telephone rang, interrupting her. She picked up the receiver. 'Yes?' she asked. 'Oh yes, it's you. Yes . . . yes, right, thank you.' She put the phone back down. 'That was my office. You'll have to forget the hospital for the time being. There's fighting going on along the Embankment by the Tate Gallery and the whole area's been sealed off by the army.'

'What is it this time?'

'Does it matter?' she said. 'If it's a big one it can last for hours.'

'For hours . . .'

She was sitting on the edge of the couch and without being too aware of it he had sat beside her, unable to leave. She was wearing a white blouse with a high Russian collar and it was partly transparent so that he was able to make out the line of her figure beneath it. They sat talking quietly and waiting. Some time later, he stretched his right hand out along the back of the couch and gently touched the nape of her neck, but she neither moved nor responded. He rested his hand there as they continued to talk, then brought it up slowly, caressing her neck where the auburn hair merged with the shirt. She turned to face him.

'Bastard.'

'No memories, remember.'

'No memories. I don't need them, I just read it in your file.' She almost smiled.

'Revealing classified information gives a mean advantage: there's no file on you.'

'That's my only point so far.'

His hand moved to cup her neck and he pulled her gently towards him. She resisted a little. 'Don't make me.'

'Never again, I promise you. Unless you want me to.'

They were lying side by side on her bed. It was quarter to six on the morning of Tuesday, March 8.

He sat up. 'I can't relax without knowing.'

'You weren't bored waiting?' She turned to watch him in the half light.

'Not too bad . . .' He was smiling.

'I understand. OK. I'll try and see how the battle goes. Maybe even the hospital.'

Without bothering to pull the sheets around her, she sat up in bed. Her breasts swayed gently as she reached forward to switch on a side-light and pick up the telephone. He moved over to play with them.

'Please. I've got to concentrate.'

She got the Duty Officer at Number Ten. The advice was firm: the Embankment battle was still going strong, and there would be no point in trying to reach the hospital for the time being.

'I'll try again my way.' Gregory reached across her for the phone, dialled a number which was answered immediately. 'Head of Station?' he said. 'This is Gregory. About my office . . .'

The call had wakened him and the CIA Head of Station was neither too quick nor good-humoured. 'Yeah, I heard,' he said slowly. 'That was eight hours ago. Since then the world's been trying to get you. Where the hell are you? I had the Admiral on the phone, mad as an ape that I had agreed to drop your guard. That won't happen again, I can tell you, girl or no girl. Then we went up scale with the President's office calling. For good measure I had one of your men from your New York office, one Mick Vanderman, hollering for you. Urgent.'

'So I'm sorry. I tried the Embassy after it happened but couldn't contact you. So I went underground for a bit. It didn't look too safe.'

'You could have reported in again. Picked up my man.'

'No time, sorry. What about Mason?'

'Four bullets, one of them serious, the other three flesh wounds. They were operating a little while ago. At Westminster Hospital, did you know?'

'Yes, and about the Embankment fight so I can't get near.'

'We'll take you. I'll fix it and ring you back. Give me your number.'

'I'll ring you. I don't give anything these days. Not even to the CIA. Not with people listening in.'

'I'm fed to the teeth with you, Gregory. We're meant to be on the same side.'

'Better tight than dead. I'll ring *you*.' Gregory put the telephone down. 'May I ring New York?' he asked. He was still lying half across her.

'Help yourself,' Eileen said. 'What's an enormous telephone bill between friends?' She was doing something to him under the sheets.

'I'll reverse the charges.'

'I'm not the one that's hard up.'

He dialled a New York number. It took him several times before he got through to the Institute. It was one in the morning there but Vanderman was still at his desk. 'Is that you Mick . . .? Yes it's . . . Mason, yes. Haven't you heard? The office was blown to bits. Mason was shot up at the same time . . . Critical. Pass the word around, will you. No I can't give you a number where I can be reached. Things aren't over-easy here at the moment. You had something urgent . . .? Oil? Did you say oil? What the hell are you talking about oil for at a time like this?'

Eileen was laughing at him as he slammed the phone down.

Thirteen

D AN LATEMAN of Associated Press sensed that the US
press were getting more than a little bored with stories
of Britain's slide into anarchy, but this one had a strong
American slant and his hunch was that it would pay dividends
to follow it hard. It was potentially hotter than other current
stories with a transatlantic interest, of kidnapped US business
executives or of strikebound American firms pulling their
operations out of the UK for good. Nonetheless he started out
cautiously to get the bare facts on the wires. After that he
would start digging the background dirt.

*AP London, Tuesday, March 8. Dan Lateman reporting:
Gregory Institute.*

'The London bureau of the American Gregory Institute
was totally destroyed by fire last night as the result of a
bomb attack. No warning was given and the identity of
those responsible is still unknown. Two people were
injured in the attack including the London bureau chief,
Sandy Mason, fifty-seven, who was working in the building at the time and is now seriously ill in hospital. Present
whereabouts of Professor Max Gregory himself is a mys-
tery though US Embassy sources believe he is still in
London.

'UK press have already nicknamed the Gregory Institute
the "Alternative Embassy", following confirmation over
the weekend of Professor Gregory's role as special envoy of
the President. Attack on the Institute is also being linked to
the murder in London last December of Professor Greg-

ory's brother. At the time this was believed to have been a case of mistaken identity with Professor Gregory the intended target but again no evidence has ever been produced about the reason for that assassination. However, British and American intelligence organisations are reportedly continuing to work on the theory that this is part of a hard-line Marxist attempt to stop increased US involvement in Britain's internal problems. Informed sources have suggested that news of Gregory's forthcoming appointment leaked and the attack was an attempt to warn off the US Administration from following such a course of action. The existence of a Marxist-backed terrorist squad has long been suspected, but the left-wing People's Socialist Coalition have denied any responsibility . . .'

Lateman had been fascinated by the story ever since he had heard that Gregory was London-bound. The White House had chosen a rank outsider as special presidential envoy and, despite Gregory's standing in Washington and his British background, it all didn't quite fit. Then, going back through AP's files on Gregory, Lateman came across a low-key report from their Washington bureau, that the Gregory Institute was involved in a British oil-research project. Lateman liked stories about oil and had a long-lived and, in the world of the big companies, notorious reputation for digging out the seamier aspects of oil supply deals. Taken together, these facts decided him to risk arrest and see what he could find in an early morning visit to the still smoking ruins of the Institute's bureau in Bond Street.

He picked his way cautiously amidst the rubble, waving his press card whenever he was challenged, until he spotted the officer he was looking for: he had recently given the Chief of the London bomb-squad a good and well-publicised write-up. The Chief Inspector even smiled when Lateman appeared amidst the smoke and ashes.

'Brought your shovel? What are you on, Mr Lateman?'

'Nothing much. A little background to this one.'

'Another bomb. Routine. Nought new in that for you boys.'

'This particular bomb has blown up part of one of New York's biggest research institutes. I have an American interest.'

'I see. Well, the press line won't surprise you: we don't know who did it, as usual. There's not much left of the building. You can see that also. Two injured including the bureau chief, name of Mason, who's been rushed to Westminster emergency.'

'I heard. Caught in the blast.'

'No. That's the one oddity. Four bullets in him. Must have happened before the bomb went off.'

'Bullets, eh?'

'You know him?'

'No, but he's close to Max Gregory himself.'

'That makes a difference?'

'You tell me, Chief Inspector. Look, do me a favour: I have a deadline to meet, so give me a break, or I'll have to go to the hospital.'

'Sorry. You won't get much there either, even if you do get through the fighting on the Embankment. They've put a guard on his room, so beware. The security boys like locking journalists up and asking questions later.'

'A special guard and you really tell me you don't know more?'

'Not me, mate. Not my department.'

'Was it the Brother's lot?'

'They say not. Not his mark. Bit of a puzzle, but who the hell cares? We don't have the men or resources to follow these things up any more and all we do is defuse or pick up the bits. You know how many unsolved cases there are; you know we don't even bother opening files on some of these bomb outrages. I tell you, Mr Lateman, strictly off the record, the sooner the Commander's boys get a grip, the better I'll be pleased. He's not my cup of tea and he's got too many associations with some of the things my father died for in the war, but I'd rather have his law-and-order gang than that bunch of Moscow-directed Commies . . . Don't quote me.'

'Sure. Nice to run into you again, Chief Inspector. Glad you liked that article. Syndicated across the States. I'll send you some cuttings.'

Paint peeled from the walls and ceilings, the floors were littered with cigarette butts, a trail of blood led across the linoleum at one end of the corridor and a battered stretcher trolley, with one of its wheels missing, stood drunkenly in the corner of the reception area. There were about twenty patients on the wooden benches or lying on the floor of Westminster Hospital's emergency wing, all of them men, all casualties of the street battle that was still going on outside. A sour-faced sister supervised the scene from behind a reception desk while three or four armed security guards patrolled by the metal-shuttered doors.

Two of the guards moved forward routinely as Lateman entered. By slipping down the maze of little back streets behind Horseferry Road, and constantly retracing his steps when he saw trouble ahead, the journalist had reached the hospital with remarkably little difficulty. Now, putting his hands automatically above his head, he submitted to a rough but effective body search before being allowed forward to the desk.

'Sandy Mason?' he asked. 'Admitted last night with gun-shot wounds.'

The sister looked up, scowled, then reluctantly consulted her admissions sheet. 'No visitors,' she announced eventually.

'I'm a friend.'

'You heard me. If you want to argue, talk to the duty sergeant.'

'Where?'

'Down the corridor, first door on the left past the lavatories. You'll have some hard talking to do. There's a police guard outside his door,' she added more helpfully. 'He's badly shot up.'

Lateman nodded gratefully. 'A lot of that infection around these days,' he said. He moved carefully along the green-painted corridor, avoiding the door of the room to which he had been directed. No one stopped him and harassed nurses and doctors paid little attention as he edged on past high piles of unwashed hospital bedding. The all-pervading smell of carbolic could not disguise more human odours, and Lateman wrinkled his nose in disgust. The red eyes in his lined white face darted nervously from side to side as he made his way past a disused lift and up a flight of stairs to the second floor. Good investigative journalists learn to read documents upside down; Mason's room number on the sister's admission sheet had been easily visible.

The Intensive Care Unit was a degree less shabby than the rest of the building but the foetid smell and the overall sense of greyness persisted, helped by the fact that half the corridor lights were not functioning. A post-operative case of indeterminate sex, with its dripfeed bottle hung precariously above the bed, lay unattended on a stretcher. Despite past rigours as war correspondent, Lateman hated blood and all forms of sickness and he averted his eyes. Then, at the end of a long passageway, he spotted a uniformed policeman sitting on a hard-backed chair outside a door, reading the *Daily Star*. A sten-gun rested casually across the man's knees.

Lateman backed round a corner out of sight and almost immediately saw his opportunity: through the open door of an empty office, a white coat was hanging on a peg by the door. On a table beside it lay a metal tray equipped with surgical instruments, sterile gloves and dressing pads. A few moments later, attired in the white coat and carrying the tray like a professional, Lateman turned back down the corridor and advanced on the policeman. The latter rose to his feet as he approached, dropping the newspaper and cradling the gun in his arms.

'Time to change the poor bugger's dressing again,' Lateman said.

'The nurse must have done that less than an hour and a half ago,' the policeman said, glancing at his watch.

'It's non-stop with wounds weeping like that,' Lateman continued at his glib best.

'OK, you can . . .' The policeman moved to let him aside, then paused. 'I don't know you. Where's your pass? You should be wearing it.'

Lateman's face fell theatrically and he moved his hand up to the breast pocket of his white coat where, he had observed, the hospital staff clipped their laminated photographic passes. 'Damn it to hell. Just changed coats. I must've left it on the one for the laundry. I'll change it over when I've finished doing the dressings.'

'Well . . . I suppose so,' said the policeman reluctantly. 'Say, you're not British. That accent . . .'

'Right. Canadian, and boy am I waiting to go home, just as soon as I've sold my house. Have you tried to sell a house these days? I can't give it away.'

Lateman put down the tray on a bench and obediently raised his arms above his head while the policeman ran his hands over him. 'OK. You can go in. But leave the door open.'

Lateman slipped through into the tiny unventilated room. The policeman watched for a moment then went back to his newspaper. Mason lay in the half dark, eyes open, staring towards the ceiling. At the sound, he moved his eyes fractionally in Lateman's direction, and raised his eyebrows enquiringly. 'Not again,' he muttered.

'Relax,' Lateman whispered, approaching the bed and putting the tray down on a side table. 'Name's Lateman. Nothing to do with the hospital. Sent by Max Gregory. He couldn't get here. He smells more trouble and has gone under cover.'

'Who are you?' Mason's voice was faint.

'Dan Lateman. Old friend of Maxie's.' When he got into the swing, Lateman had no compunction about lying.

'Maxie, eh? Must be a very good friend.' Mason paused. 'Don't know you. But the name's familiar . . . somehow.' Hoarse but determined, his words came with considerable effort.

'Don't know you either,' said Lateman, cheerfully. 'Sorry about your little accident. Doctor tells me you are going to pull through fine. You'll be out of here in a couple of weeks. Idea who did it?'

'The hell, no.'

'Or why?'

'I dunno,' Mason spoke slowly. 'A man came . . . I remember a gun then nothing more. Not until I was here. The building went up, I gather.'

'A complete write-off, records, everything. Maxie asked me to . . .'

'What did he ask?'

'He asked . . . where the oil figures were,' Lateman invented glibly, playing a sudden hunch.

'Oil figures?' Mason's face crinkled in puzzlement. 'What does he mean, oil figures?' He spoke slowly and at times his voice dropped so low that Lateman had to bend his head to hear.

'Come on, Mason,' he pleaded. 'Maxie said to ask you. Would they get the oil figures?'

'I don't know whether they got any papers. How do I know what they took and what just got burned up?'

'I said I would pass on his message, that's all. I'm just trying to help.' Lateman sounded hurt.

'I'm sorry, I can't think straight. They keep injecting pain-killers.'

'It was the special figures he asked for.' Lateman tried another tack.

'Maybe that's what Mick Vanderman – our New York oil analyst – wanted to talk to me about. He had some mixed-up figures of UK reserves to do with the Unst field and the Norslag concession.'

'Go on.'

'I don't know any more.'

'Let's leave it. The real issue is who hates your operation so much as to try to destroy you.'

'One thing you can tell Max from me: no way do I believe

that this is a Kremlin scenario.' Mason's voice again dropped to a whisper.

'What was that?' prompted Lateman.

'I don't know. I just feel . . . God am I tired.'

'You're doing just fine.' Lateman picked his words carefully. 'You know where Maxie is right now, don't you?'

There was a pause. 'I . . . d'you mean you don't? Hey, don't you know where he is?' In his agitation Mason moved to sit up and pain shot across his face. He stared at Lateman, then sank slowly back on his pillows. 'You haven't come from him. I should have cottoned on. Your calling him Maxie didn't ring true. Damn these drugs; they slow me like hell. Who are you then, Lateman? Who the devil are you?'

'Like I said.' Lateman had not wished to upset Mason and he stood up to go.

'Who the hell are you?' Mason repeated. 'What are you doing here? Christ, you bastard.' He moved again on the bed in a vain attempt to sit up.

'Relax. You'll strain yourself. I'm just a journalist, from AP, and on to a good story.'

'Lateman: I know that name now. Get out, damn you.'

'Not too excited. It's bad for you. I'm going. And remember: I could have been one of those others. I just walked in after all, didn't I? Could have finished off the job they started. Be thankful for that.'

As soon as he got back to his office, Lateman sat down at his typewriter and began hammering out his story.

AP London, Tuesday, March 8. Dan Lateman reporting: Gregory Institute.

'In an exclusive interview with me from his sick-bed today, Sandy Mason, Head of the London Bureau of the Gregory Institute, claimed that the attack which totally destroyed the Institute's offices last night and left him seriously wounded, was not, repeat not part of a Moscow-backed plot . . .

Lateman got that far, then testily pulled the sheet of paper from the typewriter, crumpled it up and threw it into the wastepaper basket. There was no story in the ramblings of a badly injured man. Not yet.

By contrast, it was four p.m. in the afternoon of Tuesday, March 8 before Gregory made it to Mason's bedside. Lacking Lateman's abilities to deceive, it took him much longer to get through the police cordons and be issued with a permit to visit his employee.

'When and why are you going back to Washington?' Mason asked when Gregory eventually told him of the decision he had reached. The patient's face was white and he looked drawn and tired against the crumpled bedsheets.

'I'm booked on the TWA flight tomorrow morning. I'm unable to get on with the job I was sent here to do, the CIA Head of Station can't or won't help me, and that charade of an Ambassador might as well not exist as far as I'm concerned.'

'How long will you be gone?'

'As long as it takes to get answers and a firm undertaking from Auerbach and Cassover that they'll back me up all the way. I'm not going to continue to put my head on the block without at least knowing who's wielding the axe.'

'I'd like to know too,' Mason said wearily. 'You don't pay me enough for this sort of lark. I'm a quiet, peace-loving man . . .'

'I'm really sorry,' said Gregory softly, looking down at Mason.

'Can't you talk to Auerbach from here?'

'I need what they call a face-to-face situation. The rules seem to have changed, as if I was set up when I came here. Even Hunt hinted at that. So I'm forced to think that there's a lot more at stake than they ever told me in Washington, more than just empty words about Britain's place in the Atlantic Alliance and the balance of power in Europe. As the PM said to me, that's all first-form politics. Now, if there was something else . . .'

'Like what?'

'Like oil.'

'That creep Lateman was on about oil. He kept asking me about some special figures.'

'I remember more and more about Lateman. Oil used to be his speciality. He was probably just fishing, but then we have Mick Vanderman gabbling away, and that's not a boy who usually gets too excited about things. Right now North Sea sources are only of marginal importance to the US . . . But just supposing something's happened out in that Unst field that the Norslag Corporation have plans to exploit, then CIA and Washington will know about it too. And that, in Auerbach's book, would make the health of Britain much more interesting and crucial.'

'What do you do about that?' asked Mason.

'Like I said: talk to Auerbach and Cassover on their home ground.'

'D'you think . . .?' Mason began.

'All right, I tell you what I think. I've been looking at Britain through a microscope for years and now I've got a gut feeling that something's kicking around like this oil story. Someone believes there's enough at stake to shoot and burn, and they did that either because they were looking for what we knew or were trying to stall on us getting to know more. Maybe even Mick's telephone calls triggered their decision to strike.'

'Answers must all be here in London,' said Mason persistently.

'If they are, they'll surface. But,' Gregory stood up and began buttoning his overcoat, 'if Washington is playing games like that, then, I tell you, I want to know.'

Fourteen

T HIRTY-SIX hours later, most of it spent on planes or
waiting for connections, Gregory was back in Washington. Among the first things he did when he got back to his
Georgetown hotel was to telephone Eileen Byrne in London,
something that in itself would have signalled a significant
change to those who knew him. Three or four times he dialled
but the line failed to connect. Then, at last and to his relief, it
rang clear. When she answered he did not need to announce
himself.

'I was questioned about you today,' she responded, attempting to sound casual.

'They knew about us?'

'Us. . .? It's *you* that's the big news. Then they told *me* that I
was to be transferred.'

'Transferred? Why the hell?'

'I'm accused of consorting with the devil.' She laughed,
though he could detect little humour in her voice.

'What sort of people?' Gregory exploded, holding the
receiver tightly and speaking hard at it as if it were in some
way to blame.

'Seriously. I've been moved from Downing Street, that's
all, into a less sensitive job in the Ministry of Agriculture.
They suggested that I was your mistress.'

'A big claim after only one night,' he said.

'Don't worry, it was quite pleasantly done.'

Gregory was aware that she was trying to down-play it all.
'What else did they ask?'

'Lots, but I couldn't say anything since I don't know

anything, do I? What else is there to say, except, maybe that . . . I wish you were back.'

A lot of static and feedback had picked up on the line but on top of that it sounded to Gregory as if she had rehearsed the first few phrases and then ran out of drive. He had to kill a host of other questions since he realised the line would be bugged.

'I . . . do too,' he said carefully. They were difficult words for him to say and he put the receiver down after them.

At first, when he answered the call, Cassover gave every appearance of being surprised that Gregory was back in Washington.

'Head of Station got a hard time from me, letting you persuade him to stand your bodyguard down. Then he reported that you'd totally disappeared. We were worried. You could have warned us you were coming back.'

'Spur of the moment decision. I lay low after the fire.'

'Yes. Tragic. How's your man?'

'I imagine you know, Admiral,' said Gregory coldly.

'Yes, well . . . I've fixed for us to meet in the Secretary of State's office at six.'

'You have?' It was Gregory's turn to be surprised, though he had half-expected that the CIA would have caught up with his movements.

'I have,' said Cassover. Then he rang off.

'You're meant to be in London,' said Auerbach, making no attempt to hide his anger. By a window, Cassover stood watching, nervously polishing his bald pate with the flat of his hand. 'Of course, we're surprised to see you back,' the Secretary of State continued. 'You were sent to do a job – for the President.'

'I apologise about the lack of warning. But there's one big question I needed to discuss with you.' Gregory responded firmly.

'I'm listening.'

'Who's using me for target practice and why?'

'That's two questions; you've asked them before and in any case you could have telephoned. There are special secure lines from the Embassy.'

'When I'm talking about my security and my life, I like to do it face to face.'

'Nice for us too,' said Auerbach bitterly. 'We laid on a bodyguard and the Admiral was about to do the same for your Institute.'

'A kind thought but a bit late for Mason. And that still doesn't answer my questions.'

Auerbach turned to Cassover. 'You got that paper, Admiral?' Cassover nodded and produced a red folder which he passed to Gregory.

It was like any other CIA report that he had seen in the past, except that this time the subject was himself. From the source markings at the top of the first page he saw it was an assessment compiled from reports out of London and Moscow. The first sentence was also the conclusion.

Assessment CZ/A/91/84: Professor Gregory: Targetting.

All intelligence sources and covert evidence point to Gregory and his Institute being a prime target. In arriving at this conclusion, the CIA Assessment Staff took the following factors into consideration:

1. The Soviet need to give the clearest of all possible warnings to the US Administration not to involve themselves further in the UK internal scene.

2. The desire by the Soviets on the other hand not to precipitate matters to an extent where (they would assess) we would react with equal force. Thus they wish to avoid direct confrontation of the US Government by overt attacks on, for example, the US Embassy in London or other American installations.

3. The Soviet belief that Professor Gregory, because of his background and contacts, is personally in a very strong position to 'deliver' Prime Minister Hunt into the US field of influence. They consequently see him as a specific

challenge to Soviet aims and aspirations in London. These goals remain the overthrow of the remnants of British democracy and the eventual creation of a Socialist workers state.

The report went on:

The covert mechanism for carrying out Soviet aims in this context is the continued use of the Moscow armed and trained Eighty-three Commando which our intelligence sources have identified as the clandestine unit charged with assassination operations. This Commando has a small, highly professional membership of not more than a dozen, whose military-terrorist capabilities are well matched by their political dedication.

The assessment ran on for several more pages but most of it was familiar to Gregory and he was able to skim through it quickly. The two other men watched him in silence. When he had finished he looked up. 'That all?' he asked shortly.

'What more d'you need?' Auerbach hissed.

'Things called facts.'

'Christ. Who the hell else d'you think is going to want to kill you, for God's sake?'

'We'll put a much higher guard on you and your op the moment you get back to London.' Cassover appeared, as usual, a shade more conciliatory.

'That is,' added the Secretary of State, moving to open the door of his office and dismiss Gregory, 'unless you want to terminate the contract.'

When Gregory had gone, the other two men were left together. Auerbach stood in silence for a few moments, sizing the Admiral up, wondering how the CIA would jump. When he spoke, he as always chose words that could be interpreted in many ways. 'I don't think he'll do any more, Admiral,' he grunted.

The other man had a slower mind, but he too knew the options. 'No', he said after a pause. 'He won't, will he.'

When Dan Lateman heard that Gregory had left London, he continued to back his hunch and flew to New York. He drove straight from the airport to the Gregory Institute where Reception told him that Gregory himself was not expected back that night, so he took himself off to the AP Bureau to argue over his expense account and discover whether they'd agree to pay his fare to the States. He hadn't asked for approval first and had some hard arguing to do to persuade his editor that he had been justified in taking the trip when he should have been covering events back in London. But Lateman was Lateman, the story was hot, and in the end he was given the benefit of the doubt. After that, he settled down to do some concentrated research.

Shortly after eight a.m. the next morning, Thursday, March 10, an embittered and frustrated Max Gregory slammed his way into his Madison Avenue headquarters. He considered that his journey to Washington had been totally wasted and that he had been treated like an hysterical child by both Auerbach and Cassover. He would have chucked it all in had it not been for an increasingly emotional mix to do with Mason in his hospital bed, memories of Lou, relics of British patriotism and, now, Eileen Byrne. He restrained himself from trying to telephone her; by now she would be ensconced behind some new desk in the Ministry of Agriculture. But he did put a call through to the Westminster Hospital and eventually got grudging confirmation that Mason was still making slow but satisfactory progress. After that he spent an hour or two working his way down a bundle of the more urgent office papers waiting for him in his in-tray before coming to the sealed brown envelope marked confidential and personal. He opened it and spent the next ten minutes reading through the detailed contents. When he had finished he buzzed his PA and asked her to get Mick Vanderman.

There was a long delay. 'Where the hell is Vanderman? I want to talk to him, now,' he opened the connecting door of his office and bellowed at the harassed girl.

'He's left, Professor. They say he's resigned.' She had been more than a little nervous of Gregory's reaction when she eventually brought him the news.

'What the hell d'you mean, he's resigned? He rang me only two days ago. He left me this envelope of papers.'

'That's right, Sir. He stormed in to see Head of Computer Section and told him that he'd failed to convince you and Mr Mason of something and that he'd had enough of being ignored. He collected his expenses and a couple of hours later he handed in his resignation, waiving a month's salary in lieu of a month's notice. He's quit.'

'Where's he live?'

'Head of Computer Section doesn't know. Maybe Personnel.'

'Get me Head of Personnel. Quick as you can.' Gregory paced up and down irritably until the telephone rang. He seized it: 'Hello, hello? Yes . . . of course it's me. Tell me about Mick Vanderman. Yes . . . I see. Personal problems as well . . . you think he had girl trouble? Well that doesn't sound too bad. Where does he live? . . . What d'you mean, you don't know? That's what I pay you for. Find out from records and ring me straight back.'

Fifteen

IT WAS a shabby little house in Queens, set back about ten yards from the road. Around one p.m. Gregory's chauffeur-driven Cadillac pulled up by the rusting gate and he got out. Stepping around a multi-racial group of urchins playing in the mud, he made his way up the block concrete path to the door, rang the bell and waited. Eventually a mousy little woman opened up.

'Mick Vanderman live here?'

'Who wants him?'

'Gregory's the name.'

'I'll see.' The woman vanished and there was a long pause. Waiting impatiently at the door, he could hear whispering in the background and eventually Vanderman appeared looking tousled and unshaven.

'I tried to get you by phone,' Gregory began. He kept his voice concerned rather than angry. 'You get us all excited, then you quit. The dossier you left for me is quite something.'

'I . . . I was going to let you know, Sir . . . talk to you . . . when things cooled down a bit. I'm sorry,' Vanderman began. While he could be excused for being taken aback by the arrival of his unexpected visitor, Gregory was amazed at the change in Vanderman. The man had never exuded toughness, but he had been cleverly glib and now he was barely coherent.

'I am sorry . . . about a lot of things,' Vanderman paused. 'I . . . I . . . Did anyone see you come here?' He looked nervously towards the street where Gregory's car was parked.

'Did anyone see me?' Gregory echoed the words unthinkingly.

'Don't you realise? It was only two days ago, though it seems like years. They picked me up and held me for most of the day, interrogating me. Then they started telephoning me at all hours, day and night. I couldn't keep it up, you know. My girlfriend . . . well I'm back with her and we want to get married.' The boy was shaking.

'Sure you do. So somebody's been threatening you?'

'I'm not saying anything. I'm not working for you and I'm through with your project, Professor Gregory. Through.'

'You . . . What did they threaten?'

'I . . . I've nothing to say, Professor.'

'Oh yes you have, Mick.' Gregory reached out and grabbed the younger man's arm. 'You and I are going for a long drive, right now, and have ourselves an even longer talk. Go get smartened up and let's go.'

Long Island extends one hundred and twenty miles east-north-east from Manhattan. Along the southern shore runs the State 27A freeway which winds through Freeport, Babylon and the Hamptons. A thick dust of snow billowed across the windscreen as they followed it east and then cut north onto the Montauk Highway until they reached Montauk itself. Vanderman sat hunched in the right hand rear seat of the Cadillac, staring blankly out at the greyness of the day. From time to time he looked round as if to check whether they were being followed, but after a while he gave up. 'Where are we going?' he asked in a subdued voice.

'One of the few good fish restaurants that stays open all year. You haven't had lunch?'

'I er . . .'

'Good. You'll enjoy the place. And the wine list.' Gregory was talking to him in a grown-up matter-of-fact way, as if they were both bound for some Ivy League dinner. For a while the effort was lost on Vanderman but when they reached the restaurant, a pleasant wood and glass building that looked out across the white-flecked waters of a bay, he gradually began to relax. Then Gregory pushed straight to the core of the problem, firmly but not to the extent of frightening the boy into silence.

'Talk it out. What have you really proved?'

'Proved . . .?' Vanderman hesitated, then shrugged in resignation. 'Well, I told you that I programmed all the figures you left me, from the oil companies and from the CIA. I pushed them through the computer again and again and each time I came up with the same thing: company statistics add up nicely to the published yield for Shetland and specifically Unst block estimates, but when I used CIA figures, picked up privately from the Norslag Corporation, I got a totally different reading. Those ones projected total Unst reserves as being many times larger than declared.'

'Defend your case, Mick. We all know the terrific difficulties in estimating how much oil's buried out there, particularly in the north Shetland areas where it's in very porous sandstone. Difficult to estimate; difficult to extract. You told me that in the best areas they only pull out fifty percent of the stuff, and in the worst it's something less than fourteen. Then there's operating depth: there's a problem over three-seven-five metres, right?'

'Right, or right with existing technology. Point two is that oil companies are publicly pessimistic. They consistently underestimate amounts of oil they will be able to deliver from any given field, since, quite reasonably, they have to plan their investment on the basis of what they know they can get. They certainly mustn't assume any bonanza without hard evidence from trial drillings, though secret figures such as the CIA get could be more optimistic than published ones. With all that said, there's still an enormous amount of guesswork about future reserves.' Vanderman paused as a waiter came up with their order.

Gregory sat back, eyes half-closed, sipping beer from a tall glass, watching the younger man as he talked on. There was no doubting the sincerity of Vanderman's analysis; he was beginning to recover something of his old enthusiasm as well. 'But not to that extent,' Gregory muttered. 'And the projected investment figures are also surprisingly large.'

'Right again. But wait till I'm finished. Proposition three is that oil companies cream off fields to achieve maximum profitability, leaving a lot of oil down there which could have been recovered if development decisions weren't taken on purely financial grounds in order to maximise their immediate profits.'

'Big words . . . And that's always going to happen?' said Gregory, pausing for long enough to pick at the plate of smoked salmon in front of him.

'With existing technology, like I said. But now comes proposition four; the new one. It's not sci-fi that sooner or later one of the major oil companies will develop a technique not only to cream off a much greater percentage of the currently available oil lying close under the seabed, but will also develop the capability of extracting oil from much much greater depths than before. And from bad rock. Overall estimates of potential reserves would then be that much greater, because present estimates are based on what presently can be taken out.'

'It's like being back at school. But just supposing the Norslag Corporation had done it, surely the others won't be far behind? They leak like sieves and the way they spy on each other makes CIA operations look like a school playground.'

'Not if a company really closes ranks and keeps it under wraps. It would be their big, big secret. But wait a minute. The other thing I did was to find out whether these surprise figures and investment projections were also reflected in the evidence from Shell, Texaco, and the other big American and European companies. Answer, no, but hardly surprising given that these figures are constantly put to so much scrutiny by Western oil experts. It would be inconceivable that something of this magnitude could have escaped unnoticed.'

'So what's different about Norslag?'

'Well, they are so multinational, with a hell of a lot being worked on at their Oslo and Paris HQ's, that they escape a lot of British and US checks and controls. And, most significantly of all, they have some pretty suspicious tie-ins with the Iron Curtain countries, particularly Moscow. What I do know is that they're ploughing a hell of a pack of money into development technology, and my guess is that though they may not be able to pull much more out of the sea right at this moment they're confident they will be able to do so in the next year or so. So they're planning their future investment on that basis.'

'Why hasn't all this leaked?' Gregory asked, though he knew the answer already.

'It has. To us.'

'And if we know, the betting is that Moscow does too?' Gregory asked provokingly.

'A fair assumption.'

'And the British? Most of Norslag assets come from BP or used to be British owned.'

'In the state they're in, Professor? It's possible, but even if they did, what could they do with the information?'

'Hunt gave me the first whiff of this. My guess is . . . but how did it leak to the Institute . . . to Mick Vanderman?'

'You guess from now, Sir. I'd go for it simply being someone's big clerical error.'

'OK, bright boy, what conclusion do you draw?'

'I don't draw any. That's your job, Professor. I'm just paid . . . I was paid to be an oil economist.'

'You're still on the books, if you want,' said Gregory sharply. 'Right: let me think aloud. It could be neat to prove some connection between the possibility – and it still is just a possibility – of vast British oil reserves and the fact that Britain itself is being kept on the boil. But all we *may* have identified is a screwed-up computer and an equally screwed-up Mick Vanderman.'

'If you like.' Vanderman grinned. For the first time he was beginning to enjoy Gregory's catechism.

'Supposing you're not nuts, and supposing the Norslag group are sitting on something enormous and have done a deal with the Russians . . .'

'Still with you,' said Mick Vanderman.

'That's a hell of a big prize to be offering Moscow with their present oil-supply problems. They would go to any lengths to ensure it all comes to them, and Washington would go to equal lengths to stop them.'

'Right, Sir.'

'An unstable Britain might help or hinder?'

'Depends who you're talking about.'

'As far as the Russians are concerned, they know from decades of experience that a little money goes a long way in a highly polarised society. So they set about creating a revolution and then hope that with a "legitimate" pro-Soviet government in London it's all over bar the shouting and the Norslag oil is theirs.'

'Enter Professor Gregory, waving the Stars and Stripes, to take the helm for the US of A,' said Vanderman.

'And that is a very reasonable scenario if it wasn't for one unpleasant fact: why didn't Auerbach and Cassover tell me all this if they knew. And if they don't know, how do we?'

'I had thought about that as well.'

'Tell me, Mick: how much were we paying you?' asked Gregory.

'Why did you really run out on us?' Gregory broached the question cautiously, since, while Vanderman had almost totally regained his self-composure, he knew it would be too easy to frighten him back into his shell again. They had finished lunch at a leisurely pace and were again seated in the back of Gregory's Cadillac, driving along the shore road out of Montauk.

'I told you: they came at me and questioned me for hours, mainly about my research.'

'Who?'

'The chief interrogator introduced himself as Deputy Head of the CIA's oil research section. He was pretty bright, though he had a couple of heavies in tow.'

'The line of their questioning?'

'They obviously had been tapping my calls. They asked me

why I had been so keen to get through to you and Mason in London; what it was I had discovered.'

'And you told them?'

'The truth: I'd dug up some strange statistics but that I'd been given the brush off by you. They seemed relieved at that. Then . . .' he paused.

'Then what?'

'They offered me a job. Said I was a bright boy and so on. Laid it on thick. I said no and it was then they turned nasty. They shot some corny line about being worried about my leaking information to the Norslag Corporation. Kept on about its Moscow links. Then they told me: work for them or they'd get me dismissed from the Gregory Institute on security grounds. They claimed that you have a deal with them that in return for getting a CIA contract your employees have to be vetted and cleared.'

'That's true enough.'

'So when they eventually let me go, I decided I'd had enough. I'd pack the lot in,' Vanderman ended simply. As he finished speaking he turned in his seat and looked out of the car window, suddenly startled. 'Hey, this isn't the way back to Queens.'

'It's not, but don't worry, I'm not kidnapping you. We're going . . . I want you to meet a man first.'

'Yes?'

'Nils Nielsen.'

'The geology guy?'

'That's what we've been talking about, isn't it?'

'I thought he was in Houston.'

'He's right here in Montauk. He's got a villa about five minutes away. He's waiting for us now.'

'Nielsen is still top of his profession?'

'In my book, he is. When he made his celebrated break with Texaco he went through a bad patch and was out of grace with a lot of people. He's not great on personal behaviour since he does nasty things like getting drunk all the time. There are some other aspects of his life style which don't suit some of these big companies, but I don't ask about morals when I want a good geologist.'

'Why are we going to see him?'

'I want him to hear for himself what you have to say.'

Nielsen was already drunk, very drunk. A half-empty bottle of *aquavit* stood in an ice bucket on the once elegant coffee table in front of him, a broken glass lay on the carpet and books and magazines were scattered everywhere. Nielsen himself was sitting slouched in a chair, dress shirt open to the waist and hair plastered all over his forehead as if he had just been for a swim. He stayed where he was when they let themselves in through a patio door.

'You bastards took your time.'

'Nice to see you again, Nils,' Gregory grinned.

'Have a drink?'

'Not me. Maybe Mick would like one. You haven't met Mick.'

Vanderman shook his head slowly.

'No, I haven't met Mick . . .' said Nielsen, making no attempt to remedy the matter. Instead, he leaned forward and poured himself another drink. 'What's all this crap about?' he asked.

'Oil. I told you the bones of Mick's theory on the telephone. Now I want you to listen to him and then tell me what the degree of possibility is. Could there be so much more out there above the Shetlands? Mick suggests a factor of eight times published returns for the Norslag blocks.'

'The Norslag Corporation's published statistics . . .' Vanderman began helpfully.

'Published figures are a load of balls, always have been, always will. It's the reality that matters, so why the hell shouldn't there be something in it? You know bloody well that oil companies are like icebergs; they only declare a fraction of what they have, since they're so damned scared that the opposition gets their hands on any of their property.'

'How feasible is ultra-deep well-drilling? Getting round porous rock problems? Could that lead to these estimates?'

'Not at the moment . . . No, not feasible now.' Nielsen tried but failed to stop his words coming out slurred.

'But?'

'It will be, soon. Any fool knows that. The real point is whether, once you drill down a thousand metres below, you actually hit any effing thing.'

'That's why I came to see you, Nils. Have you an estimate of what could be at the Unst blocks?'

'Estimates . . . I said, are a load of bloody rubbish. It depends what the hell you're talking about, doesn't it? Area, size, depth, distance from land . . . It depends on a lot of bloody things.' He paused and poured himself another tumblerful of *aquavit*, draining it in one gulp.

'Is that all you've got to say?'

'Is that all you've got to ask?'

'No. Mick's got a load of detailed technical queries.'

'Then don't waste good drinking time, Micky boy. Get on with it, d'you hear.'

Sixteen

WHEN GREGORY got back to the Institute at eight ten that same evening, a grey-faced and unshaven Dan Lateman was waiting for him. When he introduced himself, Gregory made no attempt to hide his surprise and contempt.

'I know it's not the best of starts, Professor, but I am here to help,' Lateman began.

'Help? After cheating your way in on a seriously injured man and pumping him for a story? What you deserve is to be thrown out.' Despite himself, Gregory's curiosity was aroused.

'I'm beginning to fit the whole package together: you, the President's strong man in London; Mason; the fire; and now a rather interesting new slant to do with oil and the Russians. I have my Washington sources and from them I hear it's all gone rather nasty. It has, hasn't it?' Lateman stood his ground.

'You've got two minutes.'

'Right. I've just flown in from London at my own expense, specially to see you. You see, I think you need an ally, Professor. You might not choose me, but I've chosen you.'

'You're right, I wouldn't choose you.'

'Would you listen more carefully if I were to tell you that Washington's decidedly worried about what you might do next.'

'Out, Lateman.' Gregory stood by the open door of his office, wondering what was coming.

'Can I surprise you again? As well as you being unpopular with Washington there's a Kremlin contract out on you here.'

'A what?'

'Ah . . . Caught your interest at last, have I? A contract. Not just over in nasty old Britain, but here in good old New York City. According to my Deep Throat in Washington, the Russians are determined to make sure you don't have any more chance to cause trouble. You think you're a hard bastard, Professor, but you're not.'

'Where d'you make up your stories, Lateman? Your bath?'

'Let me show you my collection of Pulitzers some day. You probably know I've turned up quite a lot of grubby stories on the energy front over the years.'

'You're notorious and disliked. Now I can see why.'

'Good: you've heard of me.'

Gregory looked pointedly at his watch. 'You're well over your two minutes,' he said.

'I'm offering you help. Give me a minute more.'

'Well?'

'Right. You think that you have evidence that the Norslag Corporation and the Soviet Union are hand in glove in a rather interesting-looking oil development that's bubbling up off the north coast of Scotland,' Lateman paused dramatically. 'Surprised I knew? I'll go better than that and let you in on something that very few people know yet.'

'Which woodwork did you crawl out of, Lateman?'

'If that's your attractive way of asking for my *curriculum vitae*, I'll tell you. Not more than ten years ago I was energy correspondent for the *Wall Street Journal*. I knew my stuff; I knew my people; I had my sources. I've still got them, Professor, and some are a lot better than your computers.' Again he paused. 'What if I whispered to you that the CIA know not only about the interesting developments in the Unst Field and the links between Norslag and the Soviets but also think they've spotted the beginnings of a split between these two. I bet they didn't tell you about that.'

Gregory moved to his desk and sat down. 'Well?' he said, reluctant to admit that his curiosity was hooked.

'Norslag and Moscow are, the CIA believe, far from seeing eye to eye on future oil marketing policy. They're Western capitalists at heart and while they sold themselves to the Russians in the early days when they needed help, now they want a free rein to sell where they like, not to a Soviet bloc market with a tied price. But the Russians still have them in a strait-jacket. If Washington could do some wedge-driving and offer Norslag a way out . . .'

'. . . In return for guaranteed Western access to this new oil,' said Gregory, despite himself.

'We have a cause the dimensions of which world wars are made.'

'What bait are you trailing, Lateman?'

'Well, my ambitions are modest. I'm after a journalistic coup that's just a little bigger than Watergate, that's all; and I want your help. Maybe you'll give it once you realise that I'm talking sense. More importantly, you'll help me once you realise that what I said about there being a contract out on you isn't just me spitting in the wind. You can be wiped out so easily that no one will even notice. You'll know better than I do about Auerbach's personal style, and that it's the State Department rather than the CIA which is doing most of the dirty tricking these days. You've given him a lot of worries; he thinks Cassover went badly wrong in choosing you and in his little personal war with the Russians over Norslag's oil it might not upset him too much if the Communists did zero you. I repeat: you may think you've still got their confidence and that key post in London, but your ticket was torn up even before you left the State Department last night.'

'That's enough, Lateman, get the hell out . . . Now.' Gregory stood up behind his desk and turned his back on Lateman.

When his anger died away, Gregory realised that Lateman's visit had left him with a lot to think about. The man had showed himself adept at building on scraps of truth and filling-in with large amounts of intelligent conjecture. His sources were good and there was no doubt that he was someone worth watching.

Had Gregory been looking for confirmation of this assessment it could hardly have come more quickly. Around eleven that night he called it a day and set off home to his East 57th Street apartment. He left the entrance of the Madison Avenue building and climbed wearily into the rear of his Cadillac. His driver closed the door, got in behind the steering wheel and switched on the ignition. Nothing happened. The chauffeur tried several times, then turned apologetically.

'The hell's wrong, Professor? It was humming a few moments ago. Starting mechanism's stuck or something.'

'I'll get a cab.' It was just one more irritation in a day that had had its fair share of them, and cabs were hard to come by at that time on a wet night. After some futile minutes of waving, Gregory, coat collar up against the rain, set off on foot, turning down 54th Street and weaving in and out among piles of refuse left from a garbage collectors' strike of which Britain had yet to have a monopoly. At that time of night the street was almost deserted but, as he passed an alleyway between two brownstones, he became aware of someone coming quickly up the wet sidewalk from behind him. He began to move out of the way and immediately things turned nasty. A tall black youth was close against him, pushing hard, and it looked like the beginnings of an old-fashioned New York mugging, particularly when a second man appeared in front, blocking the way. They had chosen their position well and manoeuvred him to the entrance of the alleyway where his second assailant became more visible: an undistinguished Hispanic with a thin moustache.

The man produced a flick-knife and Gregory decided not to argue. 'OK, OK. You can have my wallet,' he said reaching inside his jacket pocket. The men did not respond. Even when he held the wallet out towards them, they continued to advance. 'Take it,' he said and threw the wallet on the ground, but neither of his assailants even looked down, the black man stepping contemptuously on it as he continued to move forward.

Glancing rapidly over his shoulder, Gregory saw that he was running out of space; there was only a ten-yard gap to where the walls of the two brownstones converged on a rotting wooden gate. At the precise moment that the second man produced a knife, Gregory realised, in a flash of belated intuition, that Lateman had been right. They were not muggers; they had ignored his wallet; there were there just for him. His eyes looked desperately around and over the piles of garbage in the alleyway, searching for some possible weapon of defence. The men were still a couple of paces away and why they had not yet pounced was unclear, though perhaps they wanted to drive him totally out of sight of the street before finishing him.

With the gate as his only hope, Gregory threw himself at it, praying it would give. His first launch failed to make it and the two men moved up to grab him. But with a second burst of effort and by using his shoulder as a battering-ram, he succeeded in severing the bolts from the rotting wood, and in a moment he was through into the yard beyond. The men were now right behind him, and he saw that he had only twenty clear yards before the next obstacle which looked like a high and well-maintained set of railings. It was then that he lost his balance, slithered on the wet concrete and they fell on him. It was then too that an elderly man appeared at a side door of one of the brownstones, looked around in puzzlement and, realising what was happening, gave a shout, pulled a handgun from his pocket and pointed it at the two men. There was a violent sound and Gregory's head hit the dripping stone of a protruding wall. He remembered nothing more.

He was lying on a couch in a bare room. The elderly caretaker was bending over him. 'I missed,' he said, regretfully. 'Then they ran away. They ran away, damn 'em . . . The hell has this country gone to rot. The Mayor has gotta get a grip on street crime, the blacks and Communists . . .'

Gregory grunted. His head was reeling, he felt violently sick and his eyes refused to focus.

The old man continued to grumble. 'Blacks . . . cause of everything . . . can't get a decent job . . . no decent housing . . . crime-rate rocketing . . . Mayor and the Chief of Police sit on their butts doing nothing. In the pay of the Communists . . . You got an address or telephone? Here, lie still. I'll look for your wallet.'

An hour later, Gregory was back at his office. The caretaker had rung and security guards from the Institute came to take him back with them. The first thing he did, after a doctor had arrived to dress and bandage his head, was to ring AP. He was put straight through to Lateman. 'All right. You're on,' he said.

'What happened?'

'You were right. That's what happened.'

There was a silence on the other end of the telephone. 'I was backing a hunch. I didn't really think it would happen so quickly. You in one piece, are you?'

'Fair. You're coming over?'

'I'm coming over.'

'And Lateman . . .' Gregory paused. 'Don't expect too much.'

'No way would I,' said Lateman.

At eight forty-one the next morning, London time, Eileen Byrne was picked up for questioning. She was leaving her flat on her way to her new Whitehall office when a black Austin Princess pulled up beside her. A man in a tweed coat got out and blocked her way. 'Miss Byrne?' he asked, tilting his brown felt hat politely.

'Yes?' She was startled but the man's appearance reassured her.

'Security police, Miss Byrne. We have a few questions we'd like to ask.'

'I work at . . . Number Ten, you know.' It was a harmless lie.

'Yes, we know you did. We interviewed you after Professor Gregory disappeared the other day. We would have come to your office at the Ministry of Agriculture but . . . .we like to do things without embarrassing you in front of your new colleagues. Come with us, please.'

'Must I?'

'You must.'

The man in the tweed coat politely held open the rear door of the car for her, and Eileen got in. The man climbed into the back beside her and the car drove off towards the Victoria Security Service Complex.

About five years earlier, the authorities had commandeered a dozen office buildings in Pimlico and around Vauxhall Bridge Road, and had thrown up a Berlin-style wall of breeze-blocks around the whole area, a wall which had later been topped with an electrified fence. The forty-acre compound now housed the intelligence and security services, the police riot and snatch squads, the SAS and the army's special task units. Eileen knew that this was also the site of the emergency communications network which came into play every time London's telephone system broke down or was sabotaged – an all too frequent aspect of life in the capital.

The main detention and interrogation centre was housed in a squat, concrete-faced and windowless building on the Thames Embankment. The car was driven straight through the steel gates into its underground car-park, and from there, after the routine security checks and body searches, Eileen was taken by her escort to a small, white-painted waiting room where she was left alone. Apart from half a dozen straight-backed chairs, the room was totally empty. By the light switch was a bell-push with a typewritten sign sellotaped above it: 'If you wish anything or would like to use the toilet facilities, please press. There may be some delay, so be patient.' She sat there, bored rather than frightened, with nothing to read, and as she'd missed out on breakfast, increasingly hungry as well.

After an hour's wait a loudspeaker, which she had failed to notice buried into the wall above the door, crackled out her name: 'Miss Eileen Byrne. Please report to room Number

Zero-One-Three.' The anonymity of the summons helped to confuse and upset her. She had heard much about the security police, their reputation for subtle unpleasantness and the fact that nobody had ever been allowed to prove anything against them.

Room Zero-One-Three was twenty yards along the green-painted corridor. She knocked on the door and after a moment a voice told her to enter. Inside was a thin man with a black droopy moustache and rimless spectacles, the same one who had interviewed her after Gregory's departure. He sat facing her from behind a plain gate-leg table. He motioned her to sit down.

'Miss Byrne, we talked before about how you met, shall we say entertained, Professor Max Gregory of New York.' His voice was gentle and far from hostile.

'Yes. But why have you arrested me now?'

'Not arrested, Miss Byrne. Asked to assist with our enquiries as to Professor Gregory's activities here, that's all.'

'I see.'

'May I go on? Were your conversations with him totally social?'

'I told you. As far as I can remember, they were.'

'Tell me again. Where did you meet him?'

'A long time ago. In the States. Then we had no contact until he came to Downing Street to call on the Prime Minister.'

'That confirms what we understood, Miss Byrne. How did you meet thereafter?'

'He asked me out to dinner.'

'And then what happened?'

'We went to his office to get a car to take me home. He was going to . . . well his office was bombed, burnt down, you remember.'

'Yes. We knew about that. Then what happened?'

'He came back to my flat.'

'And?'

'And nothing.'

'Miss Byrne, we would like you to be more helpful, please. We believe that Professor Gregory's presence here was not in the best interests of the British people.'

'What part of the British people?'

'You answer my questions, Miss Byrne. I don't answer yours. Did he talk to you about oil?'

'Of course he mentioned it. His Institute is working on some oil project about Britain.'

'For the CIA, Miss Byrne. What I want to know is, what did he talk about oil?'

'I'm sorry, I really don't know.'

'Please don't be naive. You were Secretary of the Cabinet Oil Resources Sub-Committee and are something of an expert yourself. We would hate to have any unpleasantness.'

'I hope you're not suggesting I told him anything about the working of the Committee?'

'I'm not suggesting *you* told him anything. But let me ask you something else: have you seen him since he left for New York?'

'No.'

'Has he phoned you? We believe that he may have got through to you once from Washington, though it's difficult to be sure from the evidence. Our monitoring systems are not as watertight as we would like. Did you know that he has tried several times today? No, you wouldn't know that. You see we believe he's coming back, and if he does we would like to talk to him. If by any chance we miss him at the airport, and we have problems with the immigration officers' strike as well, we're sure he'll come to you. So if you don't feel able to help us over his oil project, at least we would like you to be at your flat, ready to welcome him. Do you understand?'

Eileen Byrne sat silent with her head bowed.

Seventeen

W HEN YOU'RE trapped in the entrails of a political plot, the only defence is the threat of exposure.'

'Sounds very unpleasant,' said Lateman. 'And in any case, that should be my line.'

'It's the only reason you're here.' It was just after nine a.m., Friday, March 11, and Gregory was lying stretched out full length on an office couch. He had slept fitfully after the doctor's drug dosage but the painkiller was beginning to wear off and his whole body ached. He paused, raised one hand and gently felt the large plaster that was decorating his forehead above his right eye. It covered a spectacular flesh wound, the most obvious result of his brutal contact with the ground the night before. 'If you want to go on with me,' he went on painfully, 'the bargain is this: no tantalising little stories put out bit by bit. But the big reveal is all yours at the end.'

'Whichever way it goes?'

'Whichever.'

'That's what I get out of the deal. What d'you want?' asked Lateman suspiciously.

'I want a step-by-step, incident-by-incident record of what goes on, filed in a way that is totally secure but that can be made public, without any danger of it getting suppressed, when the need arises.'

'Or if anything happens to you?'

'You mean "us". We're together now.'

Lateman stared hard at Gregory, then slowly nodded in agreement.

They sat and talked through the evidence with Gregory becoming increasingly fascinated by Lateman's totally amoral and devious approach. 'Who told you about the Norslag find?' he asked. 'And that there was a contract out on me?'

'One thing our deal doesn't cover and that is me letting you in on my sources. You don't need to know any more than that I have a long-standing, highly placed CIA contact. Well paid too.'

'You want me to believe that the CIA knew there was a Russian-backed hit-squad after me and that they decided to do nothing? That's quite an accusation.'

'Don't push it too far. That's not what I said. I was told that the CIA had just picked up the information, so they wouldn't have had time to decide what to do. The machine would have had to put it up to Cassover, and him to Secretary of State Auerbach, before they took a "no action" decision like that. Even if they'd wanted to, they hadn't had time to be unhelpful and besides,' Lateman grinned, 'if they were going to be happy to see you wasted, London is a better execution ground. Here in New York – even the CIA don't want others to foul their own back yard.'

'D'you know how they found out about the hit-squad in the first place?'

'I don't know details. They've a mole, I think – in the Soviet Embassy in London. They've been playing him a long time.'

'I wondered where they might be getting some of the Russian stuff they passed on to the Institute. That's where the Norslag story comes from too?'

'I dunno. More likely they've someone planted in the Norslag Corporation itself. Unlikely that an Embassy source would pick up detailed figures like that.'

'You're amazing, Lateman. How much is truth and how much journalistic guesswork?'

'As the store promoters say: "check it out". For a start, how about asking Cassover if you're still on the payroll . . ?'

The Admiral was said to be unavailable, so Gregory rang

Auerbach at the State Department in Washington. When eventually he got through, the Secretary of State's voice was firm, distant but not immediately hostile.

'I hear you've had some trouble up there in New York, Max.'

'A little accident. You knew?'

'Heard this morning. Watch you don't make too many enemies too quickly, Max, or we won't be able to hold things steady.'

'What's that supposed to mean?'

'I guess you understand. There's no future in you getting involved . . . in other problems,' responded Auerbach. Just a hint of threat had crept into his voice.

'Like what?' asked Gregory innocently.

'Like in oil.'

'CIA is financing my project in British oil. I can hardly . . . You don't expect me to stop following around a subject that they're paying me to research?'

'Don't you play the idiot. I've been sent the CIA reports by Cassover. Your man Mick Vanderman, then Nils Nielsen. You've gone off limits. Stick to your terms of reference.'

'So I am on the right track, am I?'

'Look Max,' said Auerbach interrupting. 'I may not have made myself totally clear. Your Institute's project has been strictly defined. So was your job in London.'

'Is or was?' Gregory held the receiver tightly to his ear and waited.

'Max, you've pushed us too far. The President thinks . . .'

'The President doesn't think. You and Cassover do it for him.'

'Very well. As Secretary of State, I have informed the President that I consider your . . .'

'You have informed him, have you? . . . You and the Norslag Corporation have this score together . . .' Gregory changed direction and put out a shot in the dark.

'Who's side are you on, Gregory?' asked Auerbach, switching abruptly from christian to surname terms.

141

'It's not me that's shifting sides. You sent me to do a job without coming clean on aims. I don't happen to believe in destroying a country to get our hands on a bit more energy.'

'Talking about Britain are you? If you are, you're a fool. Nobody's destroying Britain except the British.' Auerbach's voice was like ice. 'In any case, what do you think's more important? Even with your much-acclaimed British background, you've lived here a long time, and you know how important oil is to us. Iran, the whole Middle East is still in turmoil. We've got to have our other sources lined up. You may question our methods, but don't, Gregory, ever dare try judging our aims. If the British like to pull themselves to pieces that's none of our business.'

'When you start putting the boot in to help them along, that's another matter.'

'We're not doing that.'

'You're using Britain as a battleground in your under-wraps war with the Soviets.'

'Crap. We've every interest in putting Britain back on its feet. Just as soon as we have things tied up . . .'

Gregory jumped on the remark. 'Tied up? That sounds to me like an admission of guilt. You and Norslag, Inc.'

'You've gone too far now, Gregory,' said Auerbach sharply. 'I'm about to end this call. But before I do, let me remind you: the British crisis exists; we didn't make it. It hits our political, military and economic position in Europe; not much, but it does. These were the reasons we sent you to London. But we'd be fools if we weren't looking hard at the future as well. One way or another, you seem to have discovered that the sea areas over which the Norslag Corporation have rights look massively promising, with the new technology they've developed . . . And wait till I get my hands on the man who allowed those forecasts to leak to your Institute . . .' He paused.

'I'm not . . .' began Gregory, ready to match Auerbach's anger.

'Shut up. I'm not finished. You came into the picture, via Admiral Cassover and against my better judgement, as the best man available to feed back what we wanted to know about Britain, and, at the same time, to steady Premier Hunt's hand. Nothing more, nothing less. We did not seek chaos. That's the Kremlin's game, remember that. And you blew it quicker than anyone could have guessed.'

'CIA knew there was a contract out on me here in New York. They did nothing to protect me.'

'Slow off the mark, that's all. But as you're still with us, in the land of the living, let me give you a piece of reassuring news.' Auerbach's voice came across with the warmth of a razor. 'You're in no danger from the Marxist hit-squad any more. That is, once they hear – we'll make sure they do – that you and your Institute have been firmly struck off our books, Professor Gregory.'

Gregory started to say something, but Auerbach had already hung up on him.

Eileen Byrne spent seven days and nights alone in a cold damp cell below the Interrogation Centre. The food was as inadequate as the bedding, she was given no change of clothing and the washing facilities were limited to a few minutes in a communal bath-house every other day. But the worst of it all was the boredom, with nothing to read or occupy herself with and no one to talk to except the white-faced wardresses who showed no sympathy towards her. All her enquiries as to why she was being held were met by contemptuous silence.

It was something of a relief when they came for her around six in the morning of Friday, March 18. But they were rough with her, and though unkempt and demoralised, she was far from passive and struggled vigorously. Two uniformed men took her to an underground garage and manhandled her into a car. They sat on each side of her in the rear seat until they reached the apartment block where she lived. One of the two showed he was enjoying it and was grinning all over his face, particularly when the buttons of her shirt were ripped open. As they bundled her out of the car at the other end, she had the brief satisfaction of heeling him sharply in the groin. 'Animal,' she shouted at him. 'Animal.' It would have built into a nasty incident, but a senior officer turned up as soon as they arrived which prevented too much further unpleasantness. As she was brought in she noticed that the door of her flat had been broken open and, strangely, a workman was already there, repairing the damaged lock. Of her neighbours there was no sign though she knew they would be watching through net curtains or cracks in partly opened, burglar-chained doors.

When they got her into her sitting room the two uniformed thugs were called off and the officer spoke to her alone. He was a cold, military figure with no flexibility in his voice. 'Your instructions are to stay here, to do nothing and to call no one. Do not use the telephone. We will know. If it rings, do not answer. We'll know. We'll also know as soon as he arrives. Don't try to leave, don't go near the windows, don't pull back the curtains. Otherwise you are entirely free to do as you like. You will find we have thought of everything. There is plenty of food and drink in your kitchen.'

She was left alone. She sank into a chair, emotionally and physically drained, and for perhaps an hour she stayed there, motionless, staring unseeing at the wall in front of her, questioning how she had suddenly found herself involved and trapped. Was it really all because of meeting Gregory again, a man she hardly understood, a man who, she had long known, lacked ordinary virtues of warmth and humanity? She forced herself to take a grip, and with a supreme effort pulled herself out of her chair, went to the bathroom, took off her ripped shirt and turned on the shower. She felt unclean and was determined to burn all the clothes she had been wearing while in detention. Standing under the hot water and letting it sluice over her body, alternate waves of apathy and determination overtook her. Why should she worry about being forced to act as bait to secure Gregory's arrest? She was not so involved, so emotionally attached that the need to warn him came above her freedom. But then, personally, she felt herself increasingly committed to try and counter the plans of people who had offended her. As for Gregory, he knew how to look after himself, his attitude to life would offer no compunction about treating others in an equally brutal way. She knew only too well how he could use and abuse people; he had come to try to influence the British democratic process and he could take the consequences. But for herself, she felt intensely bitter about the physical humiliation to which she had been subjected. Years of working loyally for the establishment had brought her to the upper ranks of the Civil Service, and now her reward was to be treated like a woman pulled out of the gutter. So much for the once well-disciplined British security services which had now totally debased themselves to match the brutality of the streets.

Apathy was finally driven out by determination. If that was how things were, then her contract with the system, with Whitehall, was at an end. If fear was the sole remaining mechanism for the retention of power by Hunt's Government, the sooner he went the better. Britain was over the brink; from now on she would adhere to her own principles alone. Her thoughts were not quite so concise but the effect was the same. To try to regain her composure, she dried herself, slipped on a towelling robe and went to the kitchen intending to make herself some coffee. But her hand shook so much that she gave up the attempt and instead poured herself a tumblerful of neat whisky. Drinking alone and at that time of day was totally contrary to her habit but . . . a bait, that was her role, damn them to hell.

In New York, the same seven days leading up to Friday, March 18 were crucial ones for Gregory and for the fortunes of his Institute. On the Monday he received formal notification of the termination of the contract with the CIA. Ironically and by the same post came a letter, signed by the President, thanking him for his efforts as special envoy. On the Wednesday he had encouraging news from London about Mason who, he was told, would soon be well enough to be flown out to the States to convalesce. All that time Gregory worked and slept at the Institute, and when he did venture out he was always accompanied by his chauffeur and by at least one of the Institute's security guards. While he was no expert in such matters, the guards assured him that they were being shadowed wherever they went, by whom, in a strangely detached way, he could not bring himself to care. Throughout the week too, he tried various methods of getting in touch with Eileen, but her flat telephone rang on unanswered, Number Ten refused to accept messages from him to pass on to her, and the Ministry of Agriculture denied any knowledge of her existence. Eventually, late in the evening of Friday, March 18, he got himself put through to the CIA's Head of London Station, expecting another brush-off. Instead he was given the information he was looking for. The shock news that Eileen had been in detention for seven days because of him, and that she was now under house arrest, overshadowed any surprise at the Head of Station's unconditionally helpful response to Gregory's enquiry.

Eighteen

SOMEWHERE near Deptford in south-east London, around a hundred men and women, huddled in random clusters, were already waiting by a patch of barren ground that lay between a run-down housing estate and an abandoned railway siding. Others, who had sought temporary shelter from the tail of the winter's cold in one of the old passenger coaches parked on the rails nearby, climbed rapidly out to run forward and swell the numbers, when, shortly after first light, an elderly three-tonner appeared and trundled up a side street towards the site. When the truck had juddered to a halt, the driver and three masked men who had been hidden in the back jumped out. All were armed with handguns which they waved threateningly as they moved to stand guard at the rear of the vehicle, prepared for any possible onslaught by the mob. Black marketeers were hated and reviled, but this group of customers was anxious rather than antagonistic; they preferred to stand in an orderly queue waiting for the hijacked sugar, tea and medicines which they hoped to purchase. For news had come through on the network that this particular consignment was a rich one that had been destined for select areas of central London. From the distance, to the two men who sat watching the scene from the front seat of their battered car, the queueing people looked less like shoppers than travellers, each with his or her commodious bag or suitcase in which to carry away the loot.

By around nine in the morning of that wet, cold Saturday, March 26, the black marketeers had sold out and the crowd had melted away. After the driver and two of the masked men had climbed into their lorry and driven off, the last of them turned and walked slowly the hundred yards to where Lateman and Gregory were waiting. Lateman wound down the window of the Rover as the man appeared.

'OK?' he asked.

The man nodded and got into the back seat. 'Not a bad haul,' he muttered, as he pulled off his mask. 'I'll take you now.'

They had flown via Quebec to Paris the previous day and then taken the train and a hovercraft to Dover. Trusting in the inadequacies of the British immigration system, Gregory was little concerned that the authorities would be watching the docks and airports for him, but Lateman's nervous insistence that they travel by such a complex route won the day. In the event, the immigration officers' continuing strike rather than the intention of the officials in London and Washington led to their passing through unchecked.

At Dover, by proffering large amounts of hard currency – deutsch marks and dollars – they managed to acquire a nondescript product of British Leyland and some precious petrol to go with it. But it was a painfully slow journey up to London. While, by and large, most country districts had escaped the worst excesses of urban gang violence, many of the towns and villages near London and other big British cities had been forced to form their own street troopers or vigilante groups to replace the police who had been withdrawn to increase the strengths of the metropolitan forces. These groups tended to be extremely trigger happy in dealing with strangers, so the two men decided to stick to the main A2–M2 route which was still patrolled by the national security police. Five times their car was stopped at police roadblocks where there were well-disciplined searches for bombs or weapons.. On each occasion, Lateman's press-card and Gregory's US passport helped them through, the security police automatically considering foreigners less likely to be either supporters of the left-wing PSC or the Commander's UAM. But as they approached central London, the spot checks became ever more frequent and hazardous, and questioning as to motives for the two men's journey more intense. At Rochester they were held for over three hours, with the police telephoning Lateman's office in London to confirm his credentials before they were allowed to proceed. This last incident made Lateman insist they needed an escort if they were to reach the city in safety.

'If I can trace him, I know a man,' he said carefully. 'Not quite a pillar of society, but he'll do anything for hard cash.'

The main problem was discovering an unvandalised telephone but eventually Lateman found one and made contact. Guiding them from the rear seat, the black marketeer led them through a maze of back streets, carefully choosing which check-points to go through – ones where, very obviously, the man knew or could hope to bribe the officers manning them. By late afternoon they reached the centre of town and Lateman paid off his guide with a hideous amount of hard currency. They had parked by the Elephant and Castle in one of the controlled areas which the Government had set up to ensure that London did not come to a stop. Large parts of Hyde Park and Wandsworth Common had also been turned into similar barbed-wire enclosures where each car entering was subjected to highly specialised anti-bomb searches. From these points on, commuters were obliged to travel by public transport.

'I'll take one of the shuttle buses,' said Gregory. 'If I don't turn up at your office within a couple of hours, start preparing the story for the wires. Get it on record.'

'We don't have enough of the bloody story yet, and without you I won't get it. Don't be foolish. I told you already that you must stay with the car. Here in the compound you're reasonably safe. I'll go test the water.'

'She won't speak to you. Not after you pushing in on Mason.'

'She will with a note from you. What's the address?'

Gregory knew he had lost the argument.

149

The lift gates had a handwritten 'out of order' sign pinned on them, so Lateman made his breathless way up the four flights of stairs to Eileen's door. He knocked firmly and waited. When the door eventually opened it had a chain lock on it, and Eileen Byrne stared out at him, eyes unrecognising through the crack.

'Hi, Eileen. Great to see you again. Just arrived in town,' he bellowed cheerfully, holding Gregory's note up close so that she could read it.

The door closed and then after a moment opened wide. 'Yes,' she said.

Lateman handed over the letter as he walked past her, watching curiously as she read it again. He saw at once how drawn and tense she was, her hair unbrushed, her eyes repeatedly darting towards the door. An open whisky bottle stood on a side table with, beside it, a half-empty glass.

There were a few moments of silence, then he decided to act it out. 'You didn't think you'd see me here quite so quickly,' he said glibly.

'No,' she muttered woodenly, still looking down at Gregory's note. Eventually she turned and stared at him in silence. He realised that she was weighing up whether to believe him or not, that she recalled his name as that of the man who tricked his way into Mason's sickroom.

Further doubts were rapidly submerged by events. 'Any chance of a cup of coffee . . .?' Lateman started to speak but as he began the door burst inwards and the two heavies with their officer charged into the flat.

'Professor Gregory . . . I have a warrant. Do not try to . . . My colleagues are armed . . .' began the officer.

Lateman stood his ground, forced a tight nervous smile, and glanced at Eileen. 'That's the way we thought it could be,' he said.

'They wouldn't let . . .' Eileen began. She had the beginnings of tears in her eyes.

'Enough,' shouted the officer. 'Over there, Miss Byrne. Now, Professor, as soon as the van comes . . .'

'Amusing,' said Lateman, his eyes nervously skimming around the room.

'What's amusing?'

'I've been called lots of names over the years. But "Professor"? And Gregory . . . he's good-looking and big. I am just an ugly little shrimp, they say.' His voice was brittle and the banter forced.

A glimpse of doubt passed over the officer's face. He reached into his pocket and pulled out a photograph.

'Christ's sake. Jesus. I'll have you put away for ever. Impersonation . . . false impersonation.' The officer stood, puce-faced. Lateman noted that a vein in the man's neck was pulsing rapidly.

'Again?' asked Lateman innocently.

'You know what I mean.'

'You have it on record? If so you can check back. I never claimed I was anybody. You jumped to conclusions. I'm Dan Lateman. Everyone knows me.'

'You said you were . . . Gregory. I'm taking you in.'

'No. Name's Lateman.' He shook his head. 'Associated Press. Check me out. I'm well known at the Foreign Office, and with the Foreign Press Association. If I don't leave this room a free man, you've got a major headline on your hands all over the world's press. That I promise.'

The officer looked nonplussed and was losing face in front of his men. He strode to the telephone, dialled a number, waited, and then, more or less accurately, explained what had happened to someone at the other end. He listened to the response, flushed momentarily, and said: 'As you wish, Sir,' then slammed the phone down.

'OK, Lateman, you can go. But it won't help Gregory or Miss Byrne. She's with us. Oh, . . . Lateman . . .'

Dan Lateman turned. He had half a smile on his face as the officer threw a full blow at his chin. He reeled back, hitting hard against a side table. 'That was for . . .?' He hissed the words through bloody teeth, as he staggered to his feet.

The officer stood over him. 'Everything and nothing,' the man said. 'And it felt good. Now . . . get out.'

Lateman glanced towards Eileen who had remained locked in a bewildered silence. 'Sorry,' he winced. 'I'll see what can be done.'

'Get out of here,' shouted the officer. 'Get the hell out.'

Anger spots rode high on the cheeks of Dr Frank Auerbach as he read the flash CIA report out of London. 'Damn that idiot Cassover to hell,' he yelled at the tirade-worn State Department aide who had brought him the cable. 'First they let him slip away complete with a range of knowledge that could do incalculable harm to US interests in Europe. Why the hell did they not take him out or at least have a heavy watch put on him? Second, they let him pick up, as prime travelling companion, one of the top political muck-rakers since Woodward and Bernstein. Third, CIA fail to follow up British Security's idiot attempt to pick him up at his girl's apartment . . . Get that bone of an Admiral's butt over here. Like now. I want this problem terminated before the Brits or the Reds know what the hell they're missing.'

Nineteen

H E C A U G H T the shuttle bus back to the compound, but a bomb scare had blocked the road just to the south of Waterloo Station and he had to walk the last half mile. That had the sole merit of allowing him to be as sure as he could that he was not being followed.

He found Gregory asleep, stretched uncomfortably across the rear seat of the Rover with an old blanket over him. 'It worked. They were waiting,' he said.

'And you got caught?'

'Your friend was baiting the trap.'

'How was she?'

'Unhappy. They kept her.'

'Your face?'

'A very angry thug: accused me of impersonation,' Lateman laughed. 'It could have been worse.' There was a pause, then he went on: 'I could do with a shower and something to eat. The lack of gracious living's beginning to tell. I know a hotel.'

'No hotels if that's the sort of welcome we can expect. I thought it out while I was waiting: next to an embassy, I reckon your office, the headquarters of Associated Press, must be one of the safest asylums around. The British security authorities are unlikely to mount a raid on a major international news agency, even in present conditions.'

'Asylum it is. Glad to be of help,' Lateman shrugged.

The two men reached the AP Bureau in Farringdon Street by nine p.m. As soon as they were settled, Gregory asked for a telephone.

'You're broadcasting your arrival?'

153

'They'll know in a matter of hours anyway,' Gregory responded.

'What are you going to do?'

'Phone Hunt, of course.'

'Of course,' echoed Lateman gently.

With traditional difficulty, Gregory got through to Number Ten. 'I'd like to speak to the Prime Minister,' he began. '. . . Yes, I know it's Saturday. Yes, I know my credentials have been withdrawn, but I'm sure the Prime Minister will wish to speak . . . Damn it to hell . . . I . . .' Gregory looked helplessly at the telephone. It had gone dead.

'The frustrations of dethronement. Tell you what: let me take the reins for a bit,' said Lateman. He did not smile. 'Why don't you relax. I'll get one of my girls to get you some coffee. Decent American coffee. We still have it flown in.'

'You're going to do?' Gregory asked, suddenly weary. He felt then as if he had done something deeply foolish by coming back to Britain, following his emotions rather than his intellect. It went totally against his training to act as he was doing; he had become used to power but through manipulating others, through the machinery of influence. Now, he found he had only his own resources to fall back on, that he had once again to learn how to survive unaided by that power that position had given him.

'I've thought up two options. I think it's time to try to talk to Paul Verity, the Brother. But first I've remembered another source that might help. While I'm working on that, why don't you try pick up more sleep?'

'A more productive field and you might have done quite well for yourself,' Gregory said, forcing joviality. 'You've got potential.'

Lateman threw him a V-sign as he left the office.

'Remember,' Gregory shouted needlessly after him, 'don't rate your safety outside this building. They've focused on you.'

When Lateman had gone, despite the bustle of activity in the AP office, Gregory felt very much alone. He also experienced a sense of insecurity that was totally alien to him. As an academic he had never tried to disguise his contempt for journalism, particularly of the so-called investigative type. But right now he had reneged on his prejudices. It was reassuring having Dan Lateman on board.

He returned around midnight and woke Gregory, who had been dozing uneasily in a corner chair. 'I used to think,' he said contentedly, 'that CIA were the pits as regards dirty tricks. Well, these days it's Auerbach's Special Services Unit that's alive and breathing poison. But the SD boys don't have the training of the old-style agents. They're full of simple human frailties and indiscipline and the lusts of the flesh, thank God.'

Gregory, still heavy with sleep, stared up uncomprehendingly at Lateman.

Slowly he explained it all. He had a friend, playing the oldest game on earth, a girl from his Vietnam war correspondent days, whom he had helped get out before the final collapse of Saigon. He did not elaborate on what their relationship had been, only that now they were friends.

'I got her to New York first and tried to set her up legit. But I failed,' he reminisced. 'Her mother was a pro and her father . . . well, she thinks he was French, so heredity won. She moved into a good house, clean, elegant and one of the best and most expensive in New York. Then she followed a man here to London and has been regretting it ever since. She says she's stayed long enough . . . well never mind about that. I really don't blame her, with her background. Now she caters to all tastes, and I mean all.'

'What are you on about?' Gregory asked querulously. His tolerance threshold was low.

'Just wait . . . I'll tell you. The oldest trick in the trade. My friend, she's called Louette by the way, well, one of her clients is here at the US Embassy at Grosvenor Square. Knew her in NYC and now goes to her in her Mayfair set-up. A man called Bradon. He's head of the SD Special Services Unit, Auerbach's dirty mob. Not much happens, nothing special, that is. He just talks, keeps talking to her and half the time she doesn't understand what he's on about. But she's paid to listen as well as for the other. He explained it to her once: cheaper and safer for him than pouring his woes out to some high-class shrink. He needs the release like we all do sometimes.'

'And you pick up his stories?' Gregory asked, incredulously. 'From your girl?'

'Louette's not my girl, remember. A friend, a good friend. Yes, well that's the way it is. I haven't used her often. Just once in a while, if it matched a story I was working on.'

'Like now.'

'Like now. Just fed a few prompts to her . . . questions to lead with . . . and then I waited.'

'How could you know Bradon would be there tonight?'

'I didn't and he wasn't going to be. So she phoned him, told him business was slack and that she was bored. Over like a shot.'

'I don't believe . . .'

'Aw, shut-up and listen,' barked Lateman. 'That girl would be Vietnam-dead if it wasn't for me.'

A wickerwork screen with a garden of houseplants climbing it divided the waiting room. Beyond, two partially robed girls playfully flirted with a dapper, well-dressed client, while at the far end a sensational dark-skinned woman sat behind the reception desk talking quietly on the telephone. Whatever he said, high-class brothels were not Lateman's scene. But this one was as different as it had to be to continue to thrive in riot-scarred Mayfair. It flourished by catering to a remaining élite both in position and in taste. A phone call first, followed by a further check over the answer-phone at the polished mahogany door; both were necessary before they had let him in. Then there were smiles and a genuine embrace: Lateman was a friend indeed.

He was shown into a side room where he sat down to wait. After about an hour Louette appeared, bent over and kissed him gently on the forehead. 'OK, my dear. All fixed,' she said sweetly. 'Stage is set . . . lighting, actors . . . I hope you enjoy the show, Dan. But don't stay longer than you need. I'll get embarrassed knowing.'

In the past she had told him what he wanted to know. This time he was to be a spectator and was uneasy about it, like watching a member of the family. He followed her along a plush-walled corridor past rows of anonymous doors, all of it lit in a subdued pink to highlight the eroticism. A girl appeared briefly at one door, dressed in a sort of tight leather corset, and for a moment Lateman had a glimpse of a macabre dungeon scene beyond. Then Louette showed him into a small, heavily scented room, furnished only with a couch. The wall facing the couch appeared to consist of a large darkened window, like a small elongated cinema screen.

'Lights. Music, maestro please,' she grinned, and held her finger to her lips. Music there was, soft dreamy music, canned, in the background.

'Sit and watch. This is your friendly voyeur's paradise,' she whispered, throwing an electric light switch by the door, then leaving Lateman alone in the room.

The room was plunged into darkness but the picture window brightened to give an uninterrupted view of the adjacent salon: a bedroom tastefully furnished with skin rugs thrown around in rich abandon. Bradon, a big man in shirt sleeves and trousers, shoes off, was stretched on the bed, hands clasped behind his head, staring peacefully at the ceiling. Then, after a few moments, Louette herself appeared, smiling, olive-skinned, a delicate and sensuous mix of European and Oriental blood, and moved to sit cross-legged on the side of the bed, profile to the hidden window, looking down at him. Lateman noticed that she had changed into a brief kimono of soft black velvet.

The music died away and he could hear them talking. For a moment, with all he had felt for her, a wave of distaste swept over him at this five-star eavesdropping. Until he heard Gregory's name mentioned. Then he listened carefully. The girl, with a skill that would have done justice to the most

157

adroit member of any interrogation team, extracted the story bit by bit.

The man on the bed talked of many other things first: problems in his life and office; staffing; lack of funds; the struggle to deal with the CIA men in the Embassy who were so anti the SD Special Services Unit, sabotaging everything they tried to do. 'At times,' Bradon said, 'I wonder who the real enemy is.' Then his domestic problems came out: a wife, back in the safety of the States, dully concerned with family; a son at high school suspected of moving from soft to hard drugs; a daughter who appeared all but perfection; the hell of a London posting.

Bradon was gently led on to the subject of Gregory. He began to talk about CIA Head of London Station. There were problems there, of control. Auerbach versus Cassover's men: a civil war in all but name and twice as deadly because it was secret. Things were happening out of schedule and once or twice the CIA Head of Station had not come clean on an operation. He'd been caught out, explained himself, but not to everyone's satisfaction. Things to do with oil and Gregory's brother. Louette would not be interested.

For a long time Lateman listened. For a man who believed himself totally inured to sensation, he found himself deeply shocked by what he heard. Then at last Louette made her only mistake. She reached over unthinkingly and laid her hand gently across the leg of the man on the bed, just above the knee, fingers to the inside of the thigh. The man stopped talking and rolled over towards her.

A moment or two longer and Lateman stood up. He wanted no more.

'It frightens me,' said Lateman eventually. They had left the coffee long ago, and were well down a bottle of Johnny Walker. It was three in the morning, London time, on Sunday, March 27.

'And me,' echoed Gregory.

'I don't mean that. I'm frightened because for the first time in my life I feel I know too much. While I was still in the dark, still guessing, I was an irritation rather than a danger to them. Now I feel I'm moving towards the truth.'

'The truth, but no solutions.'

'The next stage.'

'As you say. I knew Auerbach years ago. Disliked him heartily and he me, but I cannot believe that much,' Gregory said.

'I don't suppose that even now he bears any particular personal animosity towards you. You were, quite simply, a problem and as Cassover's choice you were a threat to Auerbach before you even knew you had been selected . . . Pass the remains of that bottle, will you?'

'I suppose . . .'

'I know it,' muttered Lateman. 'According to Bradon, Auerbach, far from being opposed to the idea of appointing a special presidential envoy, had his own candidate for the job.' He laughed. 'With hindsight I have to agree: anyone would have been more amenable than you.'

'And he went so far as to try to kill?'

'What's death when the stakes in their secret war are so high? Anyway, it wouldn't be Auerbach personally. He just required a solution. He wasn't interested in methods.'

'They're all servants of one country.'

'You don't believe that shit, Gregory. You've never been so naive. The stakes in this little war with the CIA were status, power, ambition. You were a threat. You had to be removed.'

'And they got a musician instead. But then why didn't they follow through, get me later, back in the States?'

'Don't you understand anything? By that time the CIA had a firm line on what was happening. You told me how assiduous the CIA Head of Station was in guarding you. Cassover got in quick and informed the President about you, and from then on you were totally safe, as long as you behaved. You were the President's man, Auerbach or no Auerbach.'

'The Russians . . . the Marxist hit-squad? Everyone kept on about them. Even Hunt. Cassover was there, nodding his head, when Auerbach told me they had been responsible.'

Lateman looked hard at Gregory. He was worried that the man might lose his grip; it sometimes happened when powerful men were dethroned and they lost their resilience. 'Of course he was. It's a secret war, remember. They are loyal on that score if nothing else. Like two children playing cops and robbers, the fun is gone if parents or other children find out what the rules are. Now they're united in their desire to wipe you off their score card altogether. Thus the failed mugging in New York.'

'Cassover's not like that.'

'Nor he is, from what I hear of him. The big heroic, clean-front man. But the ferrets and the foxes are still fighting dirty away down the line below him. They remember the days of the omnipotent CIA, the Reich within the Reich that will one day come again.'

'Come on. Tell me another.' Gregory's voice was slurred with whisky and tiredness.

'I will. Here's the meat of what that man told my Louette. I took a shorthand note. He spoke so fast . . .' Lateman took a notepad from his pocket and read:

The State Department's Special Services Unit established, financed, trained and armed the supposedly extreme Marxist Eighty-three Commando as an *agent provocateur* to prove to Hunt that the greatest danger to a Britain poised at the brink was the Soviet Union. The operation was so skilfully mounted that many of the dozen members of the Commando were actually dedicated Communists and revolutionaries, totally unaware of who was financing and directing them. And so, when the State Department set Gregory and his Institute up as an identifiable but highly expendable target, there was no need to urge members of the Commando to move into action any more than they had in their other terrorist activities which included the murder

160

of the British Minister of Defence. All these actions were designed to keep things at boiling point.

There was a long silence, then 'We're running out of whisky,' said Gregory. His eyes were almost closed.

Twenty

'THEY ARE still our allies,' said the President, with the determination of a man who had been told what to say.

'Sure they are, Mr President.' The Secretary of State responded cautiously. It was their normal Monday morning meeting, the subject had been sprung on him without warning and he did not like the look of the thick folder of briefing material which the President had on the desk in front of him. White House staffers thinking for themselves again, or . . . Cassover.

'This Administration only has one foreign policy on the UK, not two. You and the Admiral's boys really should be . . . be in tandem. And I want you to act real clean from now on. I've heard some nasty tales of the reverse happening.'

'Mr President?'

'You know what I mean, Frank. Prime Minister Hunt – he's no ball of fire but you should be out to help him, hold his hand, not knock the ground away.'

'Me, Mr President?'

Report CZ 6397/181/84. Boston, Mass. Monday, March 28.
Mason, former head of Gregory Institute, London, interrogated immediately on arrival military hospital here. No, repeat no, information of value has been identified. Subject has not, repeat not been contacted by Gregory. According to Mason, latter was, when last heard, emotionally concerned over continuing arrest of British civil servant Eileen Byrne, on whom see Report No. *CZ 5191/122/84.*

'So we're agreed,' said the Secretary of State.

'Right,' responded the Admiral. Flanking the head of the CIA at the round table in the State Department Conference Room, his aides nodded in unison. It was precisely twelve mid-day on Monday, March 28. The two men stood, shook hands formally, then sat down again.

'You were speaking to Stenheim in New York?' the Secretary of State continued, an unusually conciliatory tone in his voice.

'A bundle of use that,' said Admiral Cassover, his hand smoothing down his non-existent hair. 'Reminded me he was Chief Executive of AP, then lectured me on the fundamental freedoms of the press. Even when I slipped in that FBI pick-up on his Mafia friends, Stenheim didn't bat an eye. Said Lateman was too well known to bully. Our assessment: we can't touch either of them while they are together, sitting in the London AP office.'

'Gregory will have to move out sometime.'

'We're waiting. So are the Brits.'

'Don't forget: Gregory's done most of the harm he can. It's Lateman who will go public.'

'Joint target now, Frank,' said Cassover warmly.

Later that day, CIA intercepted a routine wire telegram: 'Personal for Stenheim from Lateman. Grateful your stand and support. Story will be worth it. We have total exclusive. Regret, cannot, repeat not, break it yet. Regards. Dan. Message ends.'

The pile of blankets on the couch stirred slowly, then, gradually, Gregory emerged from a full twelve hours sleep.

'The head?' asked Lateman. He had already been about for hours, updating the story that was now locked up again on the top shelf of his safe.

'No problem,' said Gregory. 'No problem at all. I needed the purge of last night.'

By the time Monday, March 28 drew to a close, Lateman had realised that Gregory's personal crisis had evaporated. He had been worried the day before, watching, waiting for the other man to crack, but it had played the other way and Max Gregory was back in his old form.

'We know the problem, we know the enemy.' He was now talking as if he was lecturing at one of the Institute's military strategy seminars.

'It's too easy to call Auerbach and Cassover the enemies. Britain's its own enemy. They're just exploiting the situation,' interrupted Lateman.

'They're Hunt's enemies; they're our enemies.'

'Have it your way. Does it matter?'

'It matters to me. I want to reach Hunt, help pull his act together, by getting the Commander and the Brother to talk.'

'Modest ambition. How many divisions do you have?'

'My mind is enough, helped by Norslag Corporation oil. Get me Eileen out. Give me that peace and I'll work the rest.'

'You amaze me, Gregory,' Lateman looked as if he meant it. 'All right, I'll work on that.'

'Where will you start?'

'With the fact that I may just have been ignoring a clue I was given – about where Hunt's grandchild is.'

'How did you lose that?'

'Something said while I was watching that boudoir scene between Louette and the man from the Special Services Unit. I was concentrating on the big issues, but he made a remark that suggested that he might know . . .'

'I don't believe that Cassover and Auerbach go around authorising the kidnapping of children.'

'Maybe they don't, but a lot of things get done lower down the tree in the name of the cause. Maybe even SD Special Services and the CIA didn't do it. But my hunch is that they know where the child is and like things the way they are. It's an additional try at weakening the Prime Minister's resolve.'

'A hell of an accusation. You can prove it?'

'No way, but if it's true, I won't need to.'

'What drives you?' Gregory paused and stared at Lateman. 'Maybe I should know by now if it's the pursuit of the truth, money or something else.'

'I'll read you my lecture some day.'

'Are you convinced that the child . . .?'

'Look. Even if it's not true, it may shake other things out of the woodwork. An old journalistic trick. Watch me do my *National Enquirer* act.'

Lateman picked up the phone and dialled a number. When it answered he announced himself and after a twenty seconds' hesitation at the other end, he was put through to the Head of the CIA's London Station. The man at the other end, who had obviously been woken from a deep sleep, managed to control his surprise until he got the tone of Lateman's voice. Then it showed.

'The Hunt grandchild,' Lateman began. 'I've been given evidence . . . an informer has gone on record about this. When he hears, the President and the American people are going to be more than a little shocked by this particular piece of nastiness . . . No, don't interrupt me. The President's a keen grandfather; some say that he does that better than being President. You probably know the story, . . . the bigger story I'm on. But right now, unless you want me to blow this particular piece of sewage, I want that child released.'

There was a long silence at the other end.

'Did you hear me? Good. No, sure I believe you. Not a clue where the child is . . . Get on with it . . . Yes, I'm sure you know where to find me. Now, even though it is the middle of the night, I'd say twenty minutes should be long enough don't you?'

Lateman's next call was to Downing Street, where he was put through to the Principal Private Secretary to the Prime Minister. Again he was to the point. 'Name is Lateman of AP. You may have heard of me. Now listen carefully. I have hard news on the whereabouts of the Prime Minister's grandchild, so put me through to the Prime Minister himself.

No . . . No messages. I'm aware that it is the middle of the night: No, now, right now.'

After some twenty seconds the Prime Minister came on the line.

'Prime Minister, I've got a deal for you. One grandchild for one lady whom you know, name of Eileen Byrne. That and an undertaking . . . a promise that you will come here after the child is safe. I . . . Professor Gregory has something to tell you. No . . . Prime Minister. You must come here. You'll understand our reluctance to move . . . Yes, I have full powers to negotiate.'

The early hours of the morning of Tuesday, March 29 and a child was heard crying in the depths of the wood. The drivers of the cars switched off their engines. The search party strained their ears.

'Somewhere over there,' someone said.

They stood peering into the night. Again came the cry of a child, a cry for its mother.

'OK. Go ahead,' said one of the men. Car headlights were switched up; powerful torches were produced, and a group of men moved forward through the trees in line abreast. After a while the crying stopped and the child, wrapped in a blanket, was brought to safety. Then cars drove away into the night.

At around four a.m. that same Tuesday morning, Eileen Byrne was dumped from a black van, a block away from AP headquarters in Farringdon Street, EC4. She had no coat and she too was crying.

At about seven in the morning Washington time, mid-day in Britain, Head of CIA London Station received the urgent order to move to a close on the Gregory case.

Twenty-one

THAT GREGORY and Lateman were permanently camped out at the AP bureau caused little comment among the overworked journalists there, since many of them were also living in the office for reasons both of security and convenience. Additionally, the chief of bureau had been sent instructions from New York to be as accommodating as possible and he had subsequently made two rooms, equipped with camp beds and sleeping bags, exclusively available to them. Food they arranged to have brought to them from a boarded-up restaurant in Farringdon Street that still managed to produce reasonable dishes, owing to its owner's reputed black-market connections.

It therefore caused no additional ripples when Eileen Byrne arrived, alone and unannounced, with only the clothes she stood up in. Lateman immediately arranged to have her taken by car to her flat to change, to pack a few things and then to bring her back to the comparative security of the bureau. On her return she ate, she slept and when she awoke again they talked.

'The Shah goes, the Ayatollah goes and the Russians get Iran's oil handed to them on a plate,' Lateman was saying. 'The second Harrisburg disaster shuts down half the nuclear plants across the States . . . Even paying three times what they paid for imported oil in 1981 . . .'

'Nothing new about that,' Gregory interrupted. He sat, a mug of coffee cupped in his hands as if he was trying to keep warm. 'But it has given them this relentless crusade to replace their sources. With Presidential elections next year, everything, anything goes. We've seen it over their oil purchasing. If it's on the market, they buy it and to hell with the rest of the world. Morality is thrown aside, but not just for reasons of Nixon-type political expediency. Americans, otherwise honest, see it as a question of the survival of their nation and one person, one country standing in the way counts zero on that scale.' Gregory paused and looked down at Eileen Byrne, seated at Lateman's littered office desk. She had only just woken from a deep sleep and was still trying to adjust to her new environment.

'What is it you're after?' she asked, looking up at Gregory. 'Is it revenge . . .?' Her voice was low-key.

'Revenge? No, not that. At least, not that alone. I suppose it's that I want to know the answers to a lot more questions. Like who really got Lou killed.'

'We know that . . .' Lateman broke in.

'In a funny way I don't think so. They've admitted they stirred things up here. Maybe they arranged . . . or didn't stop the killing of Hunt's Defence Secretary because, if he had succeeded in pulling the two sides together, that really would have queered their pitch before they had the Norslag deal sewn up. But the precise, all-out assault on my interests . . . Lou . . . Mason. Some one person was the decision-taker on all that.' Gregory paused. 'I also still have this other gut aim: to help get this place out of its mess.'

There was a long silence. 'How long are we going to stay here?' asked Eileen eventually. She avoided Gregory's eyes as she spoke.

'Until Harold Hunt arrives. We've got one solitary chance to get him on our side.' Gregory moved away from the table and went to stare at an AP tape machine that was clattering out its bad news in a corner of the room.

'If he comes,' said Lateman morosely.

'He promised.'

'You're so confident? Why?'

'Because he knows I know Auerbach's game.'

The journalists in the AP office had every reason to be anaesthetised against sensation, but even they looked up curiously when Prime Minister Hunt, accompanied by a private secretary and flanked by five bodyguards, turned up without warning shortly after nine a.m. on the morning of Wednesday, March 30. He was shown into the private room where Gregory, Lateman and Eileen Byrne had just finished a frugal breakfast.

'Sorry about the squalor, Prime Minister.' Lateman stood politely.

'I'm here for a minimal amount of time, Professor,' said Hunt, ignoring Lateman, 'so I suggest we talk in private.'

'My colleagues will stay with me, Prime Minister,' Gregory responded.

'Just as you like.' The Prime Minister shrugged, then sat down unasked, his private secretary beside him. Two of the bodyguards stood each side of the door; the other three had remained on watch outside. Gregory took his place again at the cluttered breakfast table.

Gregory did as he was asked and wasted no time in relating to Hunt everything he knew, then went on to give his analysis of Auerbach's underlying motives.

'What are you asking me to do?' asked Hunt when Gregory had finished.

'Call both sides together again.'

'They won't come.'

'If you can deliver the Commander, I'll undertake to persuade the Brother.'

'I tell you they won't come. They felt they were let down too badly last time.'

'A different ball-game, Prime Minister,' said Gregory confidently. 'This time you have an identifiable external enemy. Auerbach's trying to do the big steal of your greatest remaining national asset – oil. Both sides will understand that only too well. Extreme right and extreme left always unite on that sort of threat as history has proved again and again. At least try it.'

'Why should I accept your advice?' asked the Prime Minister. 'What's your aim, Gregory?'

'People keep asking me that. What drives me is immaterial. This is your option, and remember we're doing a lot of trusting too.'

Hunt stared at Gregory for some moments then asked: 'Where would you suggest we should meet?'

'Your ship again: the best possible place.'

'Very well. It can do no harm.' The Prime Minister turned to look at his private secretary, who nodded in agreement. 'Maybe HMS *Belfast* this time,' he went on. 'I'll see. It used to be a floating naval museum and is moored by Tower Bridge. It's been used for high-level meetings before, so it's secure and ready. What help will you want from me?'

'Some transport and guaranteed protection, Prime Minister. We're all high profile targets. Is it on?'

'All right,' said Hunt quietly. 'I'll give you one single try. I owe it to my granddaughter.'

'Do that, Mr Prime Minister. Just that.'

Late that afternoon Max Gregory, accompanied by Dan Lateman, was driven in a Government Austin Princess through the deserted back streets of Brixton. In the front passenger seat beside the driver sat a mousy little man in a dirty sweater and leather jacket. Behind, a back-up security Rover, manned by men from the PM's personal protection unit, kept close to their tail.

'Left here, then second right past that bomb-site. There'll be a posse round the corner somewhere, so watch it, I'll have to talk gently to them.' The mousy man muttered a constant stream of directions through a mouthful of rotten teeth.

As they turned, an efficient-looking squad of five thugs, armed with clubs and chains, appeared across the side street in front of them. To one side, another slightly larger group of men, huddled round an open brazier, watched from the partial shelter of a gutted terraced house. As the Princess pulled to a halt, the five moved round the car in a tightening circle. The leader moved up as the mousy man wound down the offside window.

'Where are you going?' the guard asked roughly, then recognising the man added: 'Oh it's you, Marty,' he said. 'Who're your friends?'

'They've come to see the Brother.'

'I hadn't heard. Is it fixed?'

'Not yet. But he'll see them. That man's Professor Gregory, a Yank,' the guide said with a backward flick of his thumb. 'Here to fix a major deal. The other's called Lateman, a journalist. They've got to see the Brother urgently, so you better let us through.'

'Not so fast, Marty. You don't have no appointment so no way can you go on from here. You know the rules. And who the hell's in that other car back there? Don't like the look of them.' The back-up car had pulled in close behind but the occupants remained seated inside.

'Them's security from the Prime Minister's office,' said Marty soberly.

'What's this then, Marty? Been going places? That's not nice, is it?'

'Let me talk to the Brother. We couldn't get to him on the phone. I've to explain to him. He'll decide.'

After a few moments' hesitation the leader said: 'OK Marty. Come with me, lad. The others stay here. Out you get.'

Marty piled out and followed the guard towards the rest of the picket who were watching curiously from the warmth of the brazier. From the car Gregory and Lateman saw one of the group talking into a radio telephone, then after a few minutes both men returned.

'OK,' said the guard. 'But you two only. Your fuzz stay here or that's an end of it.'

Gregory and Lateman got out, went and spoke to the back-up team who continued to sit impassively in the Rover, and then turned and followed Marty and the guard down the street. Two members of the picket automatically fell in behind them. Eventually the little procession reached a large flat-fronted house set back from the road. Beyond the barbed wire and high mesh fence Gregory could make out a derelict, unkempt garden. The leader of the picket pressed a buzzer at the side of the steel gate and immediately a man with a sub-machine gun slung over his shoulder appeared from a grey sentry box just inside the fence.

'Who are they?' he called through the bars.

'They've come to see the Brother. Marty's with them.'

'The Brother sees no one unless there's an appointment.'

'I went through on the radio link. I was told to bring them in.'

'Have you searched them?'

'I . . . er . . .'

'You bloody well know you ought to have searched them before they came this far. Do it now.'

The three visitors were indelicately but expertly searched, then: 'They're clear,' the picket leader announced in a subdued voice.

'OK. They can come in, but they'll have a long wait. The Brother's in conference.'

The three were led into the house and put in a bare room with a single barred window, the only contents of which were a few rickety wooden chairs. The all-pervading drabness of the room was backed by a smell of drains and cabbage, while on the walls were political posters, fly-blown and torn, proclaiming the workers' revolution. Across the top of the fireplace the most prominent of them, a red banner, read: 'We the working people create all material values.'

'Wait here,' said the guard. He went out, shutting the door and turning a key in the lock after him.

'I'm risking my life, you realise,' Marty addressed Gregory, breathing fumes which rivalled the foetid air of the room.

'Don't worry,' said Lateman. 'We'll see you all right. We promised, didn't we, and there's a nice fat bunch of cash waiting for you as well.'

'Hush,' said the man, looking around nervously. 'They may have this place bugged.'

It was dark before the guard reappeared. 'He'll see you now. This way.' He turned, and the three men followed him out of the room and along a dark corridor into a large neon-lit office at the far end. There, behind a trestle table piled high with books and pamphlets, stood the Brother. He waited, silently, measuring them up, not with hostility but with little warmth visible on his thin, intelligent face. Then: 'Professor Gregory, I hear you have a proposition for me.' The voice was high pitched and almost feminine.

Twenty-two

I T W A S the evening of Friday, April 1. Nine o'clock and in normal times London's pubs would be at their busiest, but not now. Somewhere out across the sullen river a steady drip of water leaked from a rusting grey hull, half-lagged pipes festooned the bulkheads and decking while somewhere someone was hammering, metal on metal, in a dull rhythmic thud. Inside the three-ply panelled wardroom of HMS *Belfast* it was stuffy and cramped. The air-conditioning had long since ceased to function and a solitary porthole had been opened to the damp night. From outside came the many sounds of the river: barges thudding past against the muddy tide and, above that, the higher pitch of a police launch that was to patrol in constant circuit of the ship. Inside the wardroom, etchings of historic naval engagements were screwed to the walls by their wooden frames, while a glass case in one corner still held tarnished silver-plated cups and other sports trophies which had once been awarded to the long-disbanded ship's company. A further display case, containing an immaculate display of knots weaved in multi-coloured cord, matched a tinted signed portrait of a very young Queen which hung on the opposite bulkhead. At the wardroom doorway two sailors stood guard, while a bearded naval officer with a gun at his belt and a clip-board of papers silently checked his instructions.

A young mess attendant appeared bearing a tray of drinks. The two men who had come with the Brother each helped themselves to tumblers of whisky; Gregory and Lateman did likewise, but the Brother waved the tray away. Still wearing the dark anorak that was his hallmark, he was slouched in a corner chair, watching in silent wait.

An hour passed. Eileen Byrne went off to catch up on some sleep in a nearby cabin while Gregory attempted to induce the Brother to talk. At first he failed, the other man responding with grunts and apparently remaining immersed in his own thoughts. Later, Gregory again tried to question him, but this only provoked a short, vicious outburst.

'Look Gregory, I've come to talk to Hunt and the fascist leaders, not to listen to your half-baked moralising. You're not involved in this. It's just a game to you, another programme for your think-tank's computer. It's always quite a kick seeing blood on the sand through binoculars, ain't it?'

Lateman stirred uneasily but remained silent as Gregory rose to his feet and moved to tower over the Brother. But the latter remained unmoved. 'Theatre,' he said, a faint smile showing on his porcelain face. Imperceptibly his two body-guards had moved in behind Gregory, while at the doorway the two sailors looked nervously towards their bearded officer for his instructions.

'You want me to . . .' began one of the Brother's body-guards. The Brother shook his head dismissively and both men moved back obediently to hug the wall of the wardroom. 'Harmless,' he said.

Gregory stared down at the younger man. Here was someone who had grown up in the mean back streets of south London, a man who could have jumped either way; anti-black, National Front, another Commander, or the way he had gone: Marxist, Bennite, militant unionist, Workers' Revolutionary Party, and now to the People's Socialist Coalition which he led. The Brother showed himself too intelligent to be a street leader. Here was someone who knew the power of cynicism and of his own charisma; here was no time-server to any cause; here was someone who would have many enemies among the faithful of the real left. In a different era, with a different social background the man coldly staring back up at Gregory could have been a Captain in the Life-

Guards capable of earning a VC at Ypres. He demonstrated that almost feminine style of the cat that is a jaguar at heart; and Gregory knew that here was someone for whom all of his own talents would be needed to win even the most grudging respect. So he rose to the unspoken challenge presented by the Brother and embarked on what he could do best: he put his unasked-for case. Gregory had always been known as a successful teacher, a professor to whom students had come because they enjoyed listening and being provoked into thought, in part because he was adept at adding a touch of subtle drama to his arguments. But to develop his thesis he needed time, and now he hoped that the Commander, Hunt and the others would not come on stage before their cue.

'Theatre . . . the distant view . . . Right you are.' Gregory remained standing, looking down at the other man still slouched deep in his chair. 'Can I call you Paul?' he went on. '*Brother* is as old-fashioned Labour-Party and theatrical as you can get.' He moved back a step, unchallenged and more composed, and turned away from the other man, as if now unconcerned as to whether he had him as an audience or not. 'Did you know that the "sand" in my case was . . . were the cobbles of Vauxhall? D'you know what it's like having a brother? Maybe you do, Paul, but a *twin* brother? That has to be different, especially if he's killed, not on a battlefield, not even in a dirty street riot, but kicked to death by steel boots of shits like . . . And they meant to get *me*, Paul. D'you know why? Because I was to be America's strong man, the man to pull the Brits out of civil war, bang their heads together, make them see sense, make sure they didn't object to passing all their oil, in a clean well-ordered way, to their Yank friends. . . . And half of me dead in Vauxhall.' Gregory hissed out the words, suddenly pivoted on his heel and caught the Brother's eye.

'Listening, are you, Paul?' He swung round again. 'Your friend here's getting restless.' The Brother's bodyguard had again moved out uncertainly from the wardroom wall. 'Tell him I'm just an actor, not worth the bullet and the effort of feeding me to any fish that have survived the pollution of the pool of London . . . Where was I? . . . No, Paul. Half of me is dead, but the other half is going to make this game work. Christ, I am. And you're going to help me.'

Lateman watched anxiously from the sidelines, the Brother moved as if he was going to speak, but Gregory gestured him to silence. 'I've heard it all, Paul, heard what you're going to say, what your ambitions are for yourself and for your party. I've heard it all in Moscow, and in Cuba and throughout red Asia. "To be equal before the law, where wealth no longer buys its way to power." That's your aim. And your duty, Paul, is, consequently, to react to the right-wing fascists that roam the streets of London, to prevent the emergence of a fascist state. By God I'm with you there. But you took to the streets to fight the battles of the streets, even though you saw that it was a no-win situation. As for poor Harold Hunt, well, you despise him and everything he stands for. You know he's not an evil man, just weak, a man who has tolerated too long such right-wing aims. And now it's too late, and Hunt is reaping the rewards of his own ineptitude. But you see, you don't really want the alternative – a workers' state, commun- ist-style. That would neither suit your individuality nor the British temperament. You know Britain deserves something more comfortable and solid. Am I right? A fair deal. That's what you want too.'

Gregory paused to let the Brother respond, as he knew he would. 'My turn, Professor. What's *your* objective? I know what drives you. British emigrant to the States, picking up a lot of American money, from anywhere, even taking from the CIA. Then suddenly you're plunged into reality; your brother is murdered in front of you. Yes, I knew about that, Professor. I even know who did it. Yeah, the actual people who murdered him were dressed to look like the Commander's paid mob; grey-denim people. I know who set them up too. You do also. That's one of the things that drives you, Professor. I grant that perhaps you do wish to see Britain back on its feet again. The great expatriate patriot . . . But you're really motivated by revenge. In a way it's a pity that you didn't keep your "strong man" role. You might just have done the job well and you might even have got us to agree to your terms. But you were idealistic, far-sighted enough to realise that you would still be a puppet, with your masters back in Washington . . . No, don't interrupt me now, Professor, it's my go. You've made your point. You see, I will go along with you but it's got to be soon. I'm not going to wait more than half an hour. I don't like failures.'

It was then that Dan Lateman pulled himself out of his chair and went to lift a tumbler of whisky that had been left on a tray on a side table. 'You two talk the same language,' he said softly. 'Trouble is, we're not at the Oxford Union now.'

A police siren howled through the night, then cut out, and this was followed by the distant sound of shouted commands. A few minutes later Hunt with two advisers and his squad of bodyguards around him entered in company with the Commander who, in turn, had three of his own men with him. Gregory and Lateman stood up politely; the Brother stayed where he was, slouched unmoving in his corner chair. His own two bodyguards moved to stand motionless behind him, ready to take their cue from their leader. Like a medieval knight before a joust, the Commander barely glanced at the Brother as he took his seat directly opposite his opponent. His three unintroduced colleagues grouped themselves to sit in a defensive triangle behind him, while Hunt and his two advisers, flanked by Gregory and Lateman, quietly took their places to one side.

'I don't have much time,' began the Commander, in a voice that was too loud for the size of the wardroom. 'I don't suppose *he* does either. In the past we've wasted too much time talking.'

'Action it is,' said Gregory. 'Prime Minister, may I?'

'Go ahead,' said Hunt, softly. He looked grey and worn and his eyes were half shut.

It was the first time that Gregory had seen the Commander

in the flesh. War hero at twenty-one; court martialled some years later for causing bodily harm to a junior officer; labelled brute, boor and bigot not only in the left-wing press; called himself the supreme patriot. There was no doubt that he was an effective leader of his ilk. One of the men with the Commander Gregory recognised as Colonel Makepeace, with whom he had had an interview at the UAM's Mayfair headquarters. Another, who was wearing a dog-collar, must be the fundamentalist cleric, the Reverend Mac MacNair, who was the Commander's tub-thumping deputy. But it was the Commander himself, a large, impressively fit-looking man, who physically dominated the wardroom. It was difficult not to stare magnetically at the great area of scar tissue on his forehead, the result of some street battle, which served to impart a sense of brutality to his whole presence. Only the lips and something about the nostrils suggested to Gregory that hidden sensuality, gone to leather-and-thong excess, that he had once read about in the CIA's secret briefing file in Washington.

The Commander was staring hostilely at Gregory. 'Well, so you're the Professor, the President's man.'

'Was.'

'Equal to me. I'm waiting.'

'Well, Commander. This is lesson one: knowing your enemy.'

'Him I know.'

'Do you? I think all that both of you have done is to camouflage the real danger, the biggest Britain has had to face since 1945.'

'If you're going to start on Hunt's invisible hand theory, Gregory,' mocked the Brother, suddenly sitting forward in his chair, 'then the fascists and we will do one thing in common – we'll leave.'

'I haven't started yet. You listen to me both of you,' said Gregory quietly.

'No, you listen to me,' echoed the Commander in his Calvinistic bull-like voice. 'I do not intend to stay for any more propaganda. You, Mr Prime Minister,' he turned to glare at Hunt, 'promised me that you had something new on offer. You have not learned from the last time, Sir. You are pathetic. You are finished.'

'I've learned something,' said Hunt, with a sudden surge of voice.

'You have?'

'To keep a good thing when I have it.'

There was a pause, then: 'Damn it to hell,' yelled the Brother, suddenly leaping to his feet and moving towards a porthole. 'This bloody ship is moving.'

'The what . . .?' said the Commander, pulling himself up rapidly. The wardroom was indeed shuddering, then the gentle motion and the moving lights seen through the portholes were suddenly and blindingly obvious to everyone present.

'Gentlemen,' said Hunt. His wearied tone had evaporated and he was poised and alert. 'May I explain that we are on our way out to sea, courtesy of a couple of naval tugs, since HMS *Belfast*'s engines would have needed too much time to fix. None of you get sea-sick I hope. Tell your men, both of you, to place their weapons on the floor and attempt nothing foolhardy. Tell them that waving their guns about will do no good since we have the Seventh Marine Company on board and loyalty is their strong point. We want to make it a very gentle kidnap.'

'You bastard, Hunt. If I'm not off this ship in ten minutes, I will . . .' began the Commander, red in the face and very angry.

'You will what, Commander?' asked the Prime Minister with continuing determination. 'You must avoid getting worked up. A man of your age . . . a stroke might set us all back. Now, the sooner we get our joint position agreed, the sooner we will return to the anchorage and the sooner you may leave.'

To reinforce the Prime Minister's warning, the door of the wardroom burst open and in piled about a dozen marines. Only two of them had guns, the rest carried short riot truncheons.

It took about three minutes and a similar number of stretcher loads to HMS *Belfast's* reconstituted sick-bay before the street leaders and their men conceded that they had lost the fight.

Two in the morning and April Fool's Day was past. They were all gathered in the wardroom, including Eileen Byrne, who had missed the worst of the fighting but had now become much involved in tending the injured. Gregory was doing the talking, the Commander was nursing a bandage round his right hand, and the Brother, who had more easily bowed to the inevitable, appeared to be asleep, still in his anorak, still buried deep in his chair.

'We have precise evidence to back up what I am saying,' Gregory said. 'A major dis-information effort was propagated by the CIA, a two-year programme to encourage you to help collapse the Government of Harold Hunt.'

'Who ever needed help to do that?' sneered the Commander. Since the fight these were the first words he had uttered.

'No opinions, Commander, just facts. Now, fact two: you are sitting on the biggest oil reserve anywhere outside the Middle East. The Norslag Corporation, since their series of successful take-over bids during the last few years, are now the largest operators in the whole North Sea area. They have developed the technical capability of extracting from very much greater depths than ever before, and thus they can bring a vast new reservoir of oil, from the Unst field in particular, into British hands. These could, if controlled, and according to CIA and my own Institute's estimates, increase your reserves by up to eight times previous estimates. D'you realise what that means?' Gregory looked round slowly. The Reverend MacNair stared hatred back at him, Colonel Makepeace sat in a tight silence, but Gregory had the Commander's attention.

The Brother's pale eyes flickered. 'So much science fiction,' he sneered beneath his breath.

'So was North Sea oil twenty, fifteen years ago. That was

science fiction too,' Gregory retorted. 'But now the whole direction of State Department policy, as shown by their attempt to import anarchy into Britain, is to keep things unstable until they have their own control system tied up tight. By-passing a weak but basically honest President, a major section of the US Government is acting in the belief that the oil from the Unst field overrides anything to do with democracy and political morality. This time it's not the guys that everyone loves to hate, the CIA, but Auerbach and the State Department. But while the Secretary of State is the prime mover, the US Department of Energy is also pushing him hard. There's a lot of role reversal going on: the CIA are the ones that have been urging caution all along the line.'

'I don't like or trust Americans, Professor Gregory,' broke in the Brother with quiet venom, 'but this is rubbish. It smells like a fabrication created by somebody motivated against the whole American establishment, someone like you. It makes me wonder whether you've contrived this whole scenario as part of your own personal vendetta. Your twin . . . you know what I'm getting at?' The Brother's pale eyes were wide open as he went on: 'You convince Harold Hunt, which, as everyone knows, is one of the easiest jobs. Then, with a little help from that journalist over there, you entice us here. But you lose in the end, man. That I promise.'

'With arguments like those, it's no wonder you haven't risen above street level.' The Prime Minister's unexpectedly cutting interjection produced a surprised silence which was followed by his producing two identical green folders and handing one to each of the antagonists. 'In there you'll find our latest secret reports, intelligence assessments and coded data about US operations in this country. Following our last meeting came the assassination of your ADC, Commander, an operation mounted not by the Brother's men but by Auerbach's men. My Secretary of State did well until they got him too. All that did was to make sure the agreement we had reached would die. If you need proof you'll see evidence of the amounts of money they have spent here, and who the recipients are. Some considerable time and effort, for example, was used to mount an extensive bugging operation against your two headquarters, and you'll find transcripts of conversations you yourselves have recently had with some of your field-lieutenants. And it's still going on. In addition, the paper listed as annexe five in the folder is a secret report which we picked up, which shows their forward planning objectives are primarily to ensure that you two do not meet again. There's a lot more where that came from to show that Professor Gregory is close to the truth.'

The two men took the files reluctantly and skimmed their way through them. When they had finished, the Brother passed his folder on to one of his aides, and, after a moment's hesitation, the Commander handed his to MacNair.

'I need time,' said the Commander in a subdued tone.

'I don't,' said the Brother, unexpectedly. 'I'm giving you one more chance, Hunt. One more. And I can only speak for myself, since without a lot of persuasion I won't get my people with me. One more chance.'

'One chance, is it?' the Commander echoed. 'What do you want if I also give you it, Prime Minister?'

'Two organisations are in on the action,' said Gregory, taking the lead once again. 'One, the State Department; the other, the Norslag Corporation. We pool our resources and wedge drive.'

'How?' asked the Commander.

'We talk to Norslag and make them a better offer. Classical tactic in business, Commander. Your socialist friends may also like the idea of dealing with big business on their terms, and winning. With Norslag you have a company you may just be able to control and that's what you both are after. Unless you think you can control Auerbach instead.'

'Who acts? Not him,' the Commander asked, pointing at Hunt.

'Emergency coalition leading to some form of national government, and both of you in it. The Prime Minister may have trouble with some of his colleagues too, and with the House, but . . .'

'You're talking political realities and Parliament hasn't been real for a decade,' the Brother said, dismissively.

'Auerbach will be on to it in no time and we'll have more riots in the streets, even if the Brother and I do agree,' the Commander added. 'He knows how to go one stage further and undermine our authority with our own people.'

'The answer,' Gregory interrupted, 'is not to let him know. We push around a chunk of dis-information ourselves. The report you have in front of you shows how well the Americans are informed about what you say over the telephone. If you can agree on the aim, I suggest we spend time during our sail back up river working out precisely how you are going to go about it. And the first aim is to make sure the opposition don't realise that you are going to work together in the future.'

'We are?' asked the Commander.

'Just this once,' said the Brother.

The Commander looked at his colleagues, then nodded his head slowly. The scars on his forehead gleamed white and scarlet in the dim wardroom. Outside, the mournful lights of Gravesend flickered through the remains of the night.

Twenty-three

THEY'RE over the brink, Mr President. Latest intelligence reports indicate both factions poised on countdown to a final confrontation. Forty-eight hours and we'll have a civil war with the military, except for some air force units, siding with the Commander's forces.' Dr Auerbach, sitting in his usual seat beside the President, was flanked on his left by a couple of advisers. The President himself listened and nodded his head slowly. It was ten p.m., Saturday, April 2, and lesser mortals were with their families in front of television sets. The Secretary of State realised that he had, in the President, a reluctant listener. The head of state would be thinking of tomorrow, escape to Camp David, church and an afternoon spent with his grandchildren.

'Are you sure?' the President asked. 'What's your evidence? This British fuss has been going on for quite a long time now, so what's suddenly made it worse?' The inevitable questions poured out on cue.

'Secret intelligence from sources on both sides. As you know, Mr President, technical surveillance teams went over last year and they have a good network of pick-up points at the headquarters of both the United Action Movement and the People's Socialist Coalition. We know.'

'What's Hunt doing?'

'Wetting himself, Mr President. Doing nothing. Sitting in his Downing Street study doing damn-all, Sir. First of all he survives an attempted assassination, then the kidnapping of his granddaughter, who fortunately has now been released . . .'

185

'We didn't have anything to do with that, did we, Frank?'

'I'm . . . I think you'd better stay unbriefed on that, Mr President.'

'I don't like that sort of thing, Frank.'

'No, Mr President. She's back with her family again, Sir, so it's OK and it won't happen again.'

'Surely the police and the army will keep loyal to Hunt?'

'Unlikely, as I said. They'll continue to proclaim their loyalty to the Crown, but now that the run has started, they'll desert him. My judgement remains that most of the law and order forces will eventually swing behind the Commander.'

'With an extreme right-wing Government in power, what will we have solved? Where will our access to your new North Sea oil sources be then, Frank? Tell me that?'

'Intelligence and political assessments again suggest that the large left-wing element in the UK will fight pretty hard. They'll tear themselves to pieces. We wait around, then step in and pick up the bits with a big Marshall Aid type programme in return for full control of their oilfields.'

'The Russians?'

'They'll be all right if we give them a slice of the oil. I have some feelers out with Moscow on that already, Mr President.'

'What about your think-tank man, Professor . . . what's-his-name?'

'Gregory. Max Gregory, Mr President.'

'Yes. What happens to Gregory? What about Admiral Cassover's strong-man idea?'

'We had to scrap that, Sir, remember? Gregory turned difficult, got out of hand, and we had to . . . I always disliked the appointment.'

'Ah yes, I remember the brief. What did you do with him?'

'Unfortunately, Mr President, he went to ground for a while. But we're watching him now and I'm expecting to have word any moment. Once we have him, well I'm afraid we'll have to take him out.'

'I don't like that, Frank. Gentle there.'

'Yes, Sir. But you realise, such a lot's at stake, Sir. My Special Services Unit will handle it very professionally and cleanly. We can't have a renegade with as much knowledge as he has floating around unchecked. It would be disastrous for us, and for you too, Mr President. With the election coming, the Democrats would have a field day and accuse us of tampering with Britain, our oldest ally. You know how they would slant it, Mr President . . . It could ruin everything.'

'Are you sure the Kremlin won't step in before we do?'

'Well, Sir, it's still our playground, don't forget. The British are part of the US area of influence. The Russians may holler a bit but I don't see them doing anything. Once we do our peacemaker act, we'll make it as kindly as we can towards the British Commies and the left wing generally, to keep the Kremlin out of the game. Of course there will be problems and a lot of bodies lying around but it won't have been us that did that. Our hands will be clean, more or less. Peace keeping that's all. We might even get a UN or NATO presence to dress the windows.'

'I don't like it, Frank.'

'Nor do I, Sir. You know I don't like violence, nor this sort of dealing. But the entire economy of the United States is at stake, Sir. We need that oil. Where else are we going to get it? And don't forget the election date, Mr President. Eighteen months is a helluva short time. You have your second term to think of, Mr President.'

'Right, Frank. You are right. Of course you are right.'

An aide edged discreetly into the room. 'Admiral Cassover is here to see you, Mr President.'

'Can't we keep him out just now?' pleaded the Secretary of State at once.

'No, I better have him in,' reacted the President.

'But it's not his baby, Mr President.' Auerbach stood to emphasise the point. 'The CIA made a helluva mess with the Gregory business, and it's State Department's Special Services Unit that is trying to put things back in order. And Cassover doesn't see how important this energy thing is, that it's got to override other considerations. Then your election, Sir . . .'

'Well if you think so,' began the President cautiously, but he was interrupted by Admiral Cassover bursting noisily into the room.

'Sorry, Mr President, whatever Auerbach's been telling you, I can tell you the CIA don't go with it. In the last half hour we've had very disturbing reports about what's going on over in Britain. Something new, and I don't like it.'

In the subdued light of the Oval office, the three men were still talking. It was half past midnight, Sunday, April 3. 'Very well,' Auerbach was saying. 'I agree. There is conflicting evidence. Maybe Gregory has managed to stir things up. But with him rubbed out, and even the Admiral agrees that we have that fully in hand, they'll fall apart at the seams – within the day. But as additional insurance, what if I try a bit of personal diplomacy, Mr President? Suppose I fly to Britain and get together with the Commander. As things are over there, no way is he going to come over here to meet me and we've got to have a fall-back position. I get the Commander on our side before it goes too far, offering to back him right to the hilt with troops, ammunition, money, whatever he likes. Then we run him if the other plan fails.'

Cassover angrily polished his head with the flat of his hand. 'Mr President, my advisers smell a rat, a stinking big rat. The CIA have had a lot of muck thrown at us over the years for getting too involved. Well, I tell you, this time we're for staying right clear. If the Secretary of State wants to risk his professional reputation and put his own political life at risk, I am not going to stop him. But I'm warning you that this Administration will blow to hell if anything goes wrong.'

'I don't need any warnings from you, Cassover,' said Auerbach dryly. 'Mr President, may I formally ask your permission to go to London? Our insurance against future oil-supply cuts is at risk; your re-election is at risk. With the Middle East as uncertain as ever and Mexican and Venezuelan sources most unreliable, that new North Sea oil in the Unst field is fundamental. We've got a gift in that oil. It's convenient and politically secure, and we must not let it slip away from us. If we do, Mr President, you will lose the election. That I promise.'

The President concentrated his mind. Election was a trigger-word that overruled. 'Of course, Frank. If you say that's the only way. I see it. Go ahead. Now,' he paused, 'if I'm to read the lesson in church tomorrow, I should say today, I'll have to get some sleep.'

There were a lot of people waiting at Number Ten to talk to the Prime Minister when he arrived in his office at eight a.m. on Tuesday, April 5, but of them all the Commander took top priority. He immediately explained that he had just received a secret message from the US Secretary of State, via the Special Services Unit of the US Embassy in London, announcing that Auerbach himself was flying to the USAF base at Mildenhall to meet him, and only him. The message said that Auerbach was now ready to discuss US support for moves to establish a new UAM government, led by the Commander.

'The message has come as a challenge to me. It is the sort of thing, Prime Minister, that I have been waiting for for two years,' the Commander said.

'I realise that,' said Hunt quietly. 'But you know what the deal would amount to, that you head a puppet régime for the United States Government, a latter-day Quisling?'

'I wouldn't put it as strongly as that, Prime Minister. But I don't like the way the offer's come.'

'I'm glad you showed it to me . . . We go ahead as planned?'

The Comander nodded.

At ten a.m. on Wednesday, April 6, a British naval frigate, HMS *Valiant*, put to sea. Somewhere in mid-Channel, about an hour out, it slowed to a stop and waited. After twenty minutes, a powerful motor-yacht appeared out of the mists from France. Gently the yacht hove to and a naval barge ferried a group of four men from the motor-yacht to the frigate. Anastase Grigorias, Chairman and President of the Norslag Corporation, with three of his top advisers, had arrived for a meeting on board which was to be chaired by Professor Max Gregory of the Gregory Institute.

The men stayed on board for almost five hours. There were many coded telex messages to the European head-quarters of the Norslag Corporation in Paris. Other cables went to Ten Downing Street for passing to the headquarters of the Commander's UAM and the Brother's PSC. These messages were all addressed 'personal' in the name of the recipients. CIA's London office and its monitoring service at USA airbases throughout Europe were puzzled by the sudden flow of cables, all in unbreakable one-time code.

Eventually, around five a.m. on Thursday, April 7, CIA's Head of London Station sent a flash message to Admiral Cassover, confirming the CIA Station, Paris, story that Grigorias had travelled to a secret meeting on a British naval ship. Admiral Cassover put in a priority call to the President of the United States of America who was still at Camp David.

It was too late. The Secretary of State was about to arrive on Airforce Two, at Heathrow Airport, London.

Dr Frank Auerbach, flanked by four advisers and about twenty secret service agents, stood waiting. Economy mea-sures had enforced the twin discomforts of dim lighting and an absence of any central heating and the American party kept their top coats on against the mist of the chill airport dawn that had permeated the neglect of the Heathrow VIP suite. Despite himself, Auerbach felt unphased by the change of plan that had resulted from the British air traffic con-trollers insisting on the VIP flight diverting to Heathrow because of reported fog at the USAF base. The Captain of Airforce Two had, privately, also been puzzled since the air traffic control directions had been repeatedly challenged by the USAF's own flight controllers. But it was not something with which to bother the Secretary of State and there was little the Captain could do to challenge his landing instructions.

At eight a.m. on Thursday, April 7, Prime Minister Harold Hunt, who had with him the Commander and the Brother, entered the VIP suite. If Auerbach's face drained white, it was hidden under his Miami tan and bushy red hair. He went forward, hand outstretched, and smiled his smile of yellow teeth.

'Mr Prime Minister, what a pleasant surprise. You should not have bothered. So many distinguished people standing together for once. And so early to get everyone up . . .'

Harold Hunt spoke quietly but his voice had taken on an unusual vigour: 'Mr Secretary of State, this building is surrounded by troops loyal to the British Government. Your plane is also surrounded and its crew have been disarmed. I would be grateful if you would advise your security personnel that they should on no account attempt to draw their weapons, otherwise the consequences could be extremely grave. I have to advise you further that, because of the behaviour of the official and unofficial services of the United States State Department, your presence in this country is unwelcome. You and your party are to return directly to your aircraft. Flight clearance has already been given for you to take off, after refuelling, for the United States.'

Auerbach took a step backwards and the Secret Service men closed in around him, but no weapons were drawn.

'Our first intention was to detain you on the basis of various charges, but the Foreign Office, the Attorney General and the Law Officers of the Crown strongly advised against such action. Subsequently, I spoke on the telephone with your President in Washington while you were in flight. I informed him that in the conduct of its foreign affairs, the State Department had, with your authority, gone to extremes in interfering in the internal affairs of this country. Most of the detail came, I believe, as a genuine and distinct surprise to the President and he claimed to be shocked by it. I also reminded him of his electorate, as one politician to another.'

'What the hell's all this?' exploded the Secretary of State, regaining some brief composure. 'What are you on about, Prime Minister? Is this Gregory . . .?'

'No charges for our benefit, Dr Auerbach. We have irrefutable evidence of an attempt of major dimensions to try to take over oil resources which rightfully belong to the United Kingdom. We have evidence of many of the illegal activities perpetrated by members of your Embassy and other agencies in London against the democratically elected Government of this country. At this moment certain US agents have been detained for questioning by our security forces.'

'This is the grossest breach of all diplomatic courtesies.' Auerbach, disguising bewilderment with fury, banged his fist into the palm of his hand to emphasise his point.

'Diplomatic practices have been unilaterally ignored by the United States Government over a period of several years. As your President realises, that argument would not hold for long if it were exposed to international opinion and its effect on your other Western allies would be equally devastating. The decision I have just announced is one taken by the full Cabinet of the National Coalition, which met for the first time late yesterday afternoon. These and other measures adopted by it will help ensure the continuance of an effective United Kingdom Government, free from the machinations of those who wish to pervert the democratic process.'

'Very dramatic . . .' the Secretary of State began, then changed tack. 'Mr Hunt, you will go down in history as one of the weakest Prime Ministers that Great Britain has ever known. You have presided over the destruction of a nation, you and those . . . those street leaders whom you now call your coalition allies. What the hell d'you think the real democratic countries of the world will think?'

'Democracy is a word that comes badly from you, Dr Auerbach. Your President is coming round to sharing this view. He promised me that he would consider carefully what I had said, and if he acts as I think he will, you in turn may find you have a limited future role.'

'We'll see when I get back to Washington. Without US support and trade, we'll cut you off like . . .'

'I have already agreed with your President that you will do no such thing, Dr Auerbach. We have currently both decided to keep the nature and extent of Anglo-American differences a closely guarded secret. We have too much evidence of several actual assassinations and kidnappings, including one in my own family, and the President knows that to pursue such a course of retaliation would immediately lead to our making public all the information at our disposal. Then, Dr Auerbach, you and your Administration would not last twenty-four hours. You have adopted policies that make Watergate look like child's-play.'

The Prime Minister paused and looked at his watch. 'By now your plane will have refuelled,' he said. 'You have immediate flight clearance.'

Twenty-four

I'M ALMOST ready to file,' said Dan Lateman with satisfaction. 'Then I book my flight out, to New York, I think, rather than Washington. Until things cool a bit and I get that Pulitzer nomination.'

'They may try to stop you, even Hunt may, and until the story breaks any of us could end up with concrete boots on. Only once it's out are we safe. American democracy will see to that,' responded Gregory.

'And me?' asked Eileen Byrne quietly. 'Will American democracy look after me?'

'You look pretty down, Eileen,' said Lateman. 'Where's that elation we've just earned ourselves?'

'You're talking, both of you, as if it's all over, when you know it's hardly begun. You, Dan, are going to have to live and work on that story for a long time yet. And Max . . . Max, I know where you're going.'

'I hope he's taking you with him,' said Lateman with a grin. He paused and then turned serious. 'Say what is this? This is happiness hour, which reminds me: let's have a drink.' He moved towards the corner of his office.

Eileen Byrne spoke first. 'Not yet, Dan. Don't you realise that Max is only halfway there. He's still got his own personal vendetta.'

'Leave Lou in peace, Max,' said Lateman softly. 'It's too late now.'

'Not for my peace,' Gregory interrupted. 'I have to know who arranged the killing.'

'I'll dig around when I get to New York . . .' began Lateman.

'There's no need,' said Eileen, suddenly resigned.

'What d'you mean?'

'The man you talked about: Bradon, the head of Auerbach's Special Operation in the Embassy . . .'

'Eileen . . .' Lateman came forward to her. 'Give him a break. It's all old now. Leave it.' He put his hand out towards her.

'Don't. It won't go away otherwise.' Eileen stood up and moved to stand with her back to the others, facing a wall on which hung a large map of the UK. 'What you were talking about, Max, your unanswered questions, I'll tell you,' she said. 'I don't like revenge. Even after all that's happened,' her voice was quiet and the only noise in the room came from the tape machine. Gregory and Lateman stood waiting, wondering what was coming. 'When you first told me about your brother, Lou, I pretended I didn't know. There was enough bitterness in you already and it wasn't for me to add to it. But I *did* know. The security report on the murder came across my desk in Downing Street long before I met you again. I was Secretary of the Cabinet Sub-Committee on oil. I saw everything that related, including reports on you.'

'Go on, Eileen.' Gregory moved to stand close to her, watching her every movement.

'It was a mistake. They wanted you.' She paused.

'We knew that.' Gregory hardly appeared to be breathing. The knuckles of his clenched hands showed white. He stood looking at the girl, eyes burning. She was still standing staring at the wall map.

'British Intelligence . . . the report I saw, the Head of CIA London Station . . . He had lost a paper with your name on it.'

'I know that too. Cassover told me.' Gregory hissed out the words.

'He didn't lose it. It was taken by the opposition, the man Bradon. He had no precise orders, but he knew the overall aim. A bunch of his tame thugs did the rest.'

Gregory laid his hand on her shoulder as if to turn her to face him, but she shook him off. 'Your appointment was a huge threat to his strategy. By getting rid of you before you were even appointed, he tried to prove that the idea wouldn't work. He arranged things so that the responsibility would look like the work of one of the street factions. Even when you came over, he didn't give up. He tried to remove you by firing your Institute and getting at Mason. He couldn't go directly for you, could he?'

There was a long silence. Lateman looked across at Gregory wondering whether he would hold his control. But when eventually he spoke, Gregory's voice was outwardly calm. 'If this is true, why didn't the British say something?' he asked.

'Hunt decided to wait and see what happened. It's always useful to know that there are serious splits in the opposition, to sit on the truth until it's needed.' She faced him straight on and her eyes were wet. 'Now you'll go and win or lose. One way or other it will be final.'

'You'd blame me?' Gregory was staring out beyond the net curtains that draped the windows.

'I would not,' she said softly.

He left the AP building at five past midnight on Saturday, April 9. From Farringdon Street he drove across London towards Eaton Square where, eventually, he found an unvandalised call-box. He rang Bradon's private number which Lateman had got for him from his girlfriend Louette.

'My name's Gregory. I have something urgent for you. Yes . . . Now. I'll come to your house . . . Yes, alone.' He replaced the receiver, returned to the car and jumped in.

The elegant four-storey town house stood halfway along a quiet side street. The hall light was the only one showing. Gregory went to the door, rang the bell and a still sleep-ridden Bradon, in dressing-gown and pyjamas, opened up immediately. Gregory held a gun in his right hand.

'Out,' he said.

'But . . .' began the man.

'Quick as you like.' Gregory gestured sideways with the gun and the man moved, shutting the door behind him. 'Now, into the car. You're driving.'

They moved away at once. They had reached the end of the street when two police cars, sirens wailing, appeared behind them at the far end and screeched up to stop in front of the house.

'Fast, but not quite enough,' said Gregory. 'I thought you'd get some help in.'

'What is this? Where are you taking me?'

'You'll discover.'

They made towards Fulham and, on Gregory's instructions, Bradon drove until they reached a cul-de-sac beside a derelict building site.

'This'll do,' said Gregory. 'Now, get out.'

The two men left the car, Gregory covering Bradon with the gun. He ordered him down a narrow alleyway until they could go no further. 'Turn round,' he rasped. He was fighting to keep control, to stop himself wasting the other man there and then.

'Face me. Now we're going to talk. You may briefly think that I'm not in earnest. If you do, let me tell you I know who ordered the killing, the death of my brother.'

'I don't know what . . .' Bradon began. His words dried in his mouth as Gregory brought his gun up.

'No time for that. None. We're going to talk. Then . . . I may kill you or I may not.'

Twenty-five

GRADUALLY OVER that next week, an unaccustomed peace returned to the battered streets of London. There were still reports of some sporadic gang violence in Manchester, Liverpool and Glasgow, but elsewhere, British society was learning to breathe once again.

Around seven thirty a.m. London time, on Sunday, April 17, Gregory was driving, unescorted and with Eileen Byrne beside him, to meet Lateman at AP headquarters to discuss their next moves, prior to Gregory leaving for Paris later that day. He was not by nature incautious, but with the main British groups now onside and the American security machine in Britain thrown into such disorder, he felt safer than he had done for some considerable time.

At the end of an almost deserted Fleet Street, a uniformed policeman wearing a riot helmet and a perspex face-shield appeared in front of them and waved the car down. An imposing red and black Government crest was stuck to the centre of the windscreen of the official car which Hunt had arranged for Gregory to have, so the policeman saluted them, then explained: Farringdon Street was blocked by extremist demonstrators who were gathering for a protest meeting against the formation of the National Coalition. He suggested that it would be much better to cut up by St Bride's and Shoe Lane. Gregory thanked the policeman and turned off as he had been advised.

Inside the car she was questioning him. 'What did you do to Bradon?' she asked cautiously.

'He'll live . . . I think.'

'So how long will you be in Paris?' She said it as if she did not care.

'Depends,' he answered enigmatically.

'On what?'

'On you,' he said. He did not take his eyes from the road as he spoke.

She threw a quick glance at him. 'How am I meant to take that?'

He was about to respond, but then: 'The hell. Look at that.' Ahead of them a small group of men had heaped cobblestones in a menacing pile beside an almost gutted car that burned fiercely beside a mound of smouldering tyres. A youth, aged not more than fourteen or fifteen, detached himself from the rest, ran forward, and threw something towards them on to the litter-strewn tarmac. The Molotov cocktail splintered and spewed in a wide sheet of flame.

'It's a Sunday morning. A bit early for demos,' she said easily.

What happened happened quickly. They were halfway up a Shoe Lane lined with desolate office blocks, the ground-floor windows of which were covered with the universal steel-mesh shuttering and the doors and gates barred and chained. 'Yes, that worries me. We'll back up and get out,' responded Gregory. He looked in the rear-view mirror. 'Hell. There's another pack coming up behind us.'

Eileen turned in her seat to look. 'Only four or five men. Nothing to worry about,' she said. 'Pull into the side. They'll leave us alone.'

Close cropped young men in brushed grey denim, seventy-five, fifty yards away, advancing in two packs in an ever-increasing trap. The familiar triggered Gregory's mind as he remembered other jackals with steel-capped boots stalking their prey in a Lambeth back street. Suddenly he knew why they were there. He clipped the car into gear and screeched round in a three point turn to face the way they had come.

'What are you doing?' Eileen's voice rose to a sudden pitch of fear.

'One barrier ahead. Only a handful behind.'

'I tell you: they won't touch us.'

'You said it. It's too early for a demo but not for a scissors trap.'

'You don't . . .?' Eileen's voice choked into silence as a further petrol bomb burst in a spatter of glass and flame a hundred feet in front of them. The youths paced towards them, sticks and chains dropping from their hands in prehensile menace.

'Get down as low as you can, and pull something over your head. I'm going at them.'

Gregory waited until the men came a little closer, then plunged his foot hard on the accelerator and shot up through the gears. The car leapt forward, straight at the advancing youths. He made no attempt to avoid them but deliberately bulldozed straight at the middle of the group. He had a fleeting impression of chains flailing and a brick hurled at the car, but whether it was that or the flattened face of a man which pulped against the windscreen and smashed it he would never know. The glass went opaque and he had to clear a hole in it with his clenched fist. Then a burst of shots from behind led to more splintering glass and to the car lurching as the tyres were shot out. He kept going, broadsliding desperately from side to side down the narrow street and managed to fishtail round a corner, just out of sight of the pursuers, before hitting a lamp-post and stalling.

'Out,' he yelled. 'Keep low.'

She sat up, shaking her jacket clear of a cascade of glass crystals from the shattered windscreen. They leapt out of the car together and ran down the street, away from the mob. She lost one shoe and kicked the other off to run barefoot, easily keeping pace with Gregory. Then the policeman who had redirected them was blocking their way, a sub-machine gun at his waist. His riot helmet had its visor pulled down making him look like some sinister medieval knight. He raised his gun and there could be no doubt of his intention. Gregory and Eileen hesitated, stopped, then raised their hands above their heads.

'They're after us,' Gregory shouted too loudly at the man, as if he would not understand. 'We're working with the Government . . . the Prime Minister. I have a pass.' He moved his hand towards his pocket.

'Up . . . right up. Keep 'em there,' the policeman barked back. Despite the riot mask, Gregory could sense the man's nervousness.

'I tell you, they're after us. They're going to kill . . .'

'That's right,' said the policeman.

Gregory threw a look behind at the pack of youths which had turned the corner and was advancing on them, pacing, spaced well out. After his tornado drive through their midst, he could hope for no mercy, and with a choice like that a nervous policeman with a sub-machine gun was the best of zero options.

'Run and keep running,' he shouted at Eileen, as he charged, head down and zigzagging, rugby style. A spatter of bullets erupted, tearing his right shoulder in hideous pain. But his maddened momentum kept him going till he hit the policeman straight on, knocking the gun sideways and snatching it with his uninjured hand from the man's grasp. Then, without pause, he whirled, gun spewing flame. The policeman fell in a bloody heap. Checking the gun tight against his side but with his vision partly obscured by sweat and blood from a pulsing gash on his temple, Gregory kept his finger on the trigger and backed away from the remnants of his attackers.

Glancing downwards, he just avoided tripping over Eileen's body which lay very still on the tarmac. Fighting the bitter pain, he forced the gun under his upper arm, bent low and caught hold of her. Then, slowly and unchecked, he started dragging her to the partial safety of a concrete loading bay which projected from the rear entrance of one of the newspaper offices that fronted on Fleet Street. Once in the lee of the bay he crouched protectively over her inert body and prepared to meet them.

After some moments, eight or ten of them cautiously emerged from various refuges, and regrouped to search for him. He waited nearly too long before standing and showing himself, firing until the magazine was empty. That moment came at almost the same instant he blacked out and fell, spreadeagled, across Eileen Byrne's body.

Paramedics, red crosses gleaming on their white-domed helmets, arrived with stretchers. They wore oxygen masks against the tear gas that still lingered in the streets. They loaded the living and the dead into battered ambulances and drove them away down the now deserted street.

When Lateman was ushered into the study, the Prime Minister showed little pleasure at seeing him again.

'I only agreed to see you because . . .' began Hunt, making no effort to rise from behind his desk.

'Where's Gregory? What happened to him?'

'Uh?'

'Gregory. Max Gregory, and the girl?' Lateman hesitated, then sat down unasked.

'Ah yes, the girl.'

'Well?'

'To tell you the truth, Mr Lateman, I don't know. I really don't know.'

'But you knew Gregory disappeared after this morning's Shoe Lane riot? You knew, didn't you?'

'Yes, I heard he and the girl had lost themselves. Tragic . . . but I don't know where he is now. Why . . . why don't you ask your Washington friends?'

'I have and they don't have him.'

Hunt moved to the attack. 'Why are you so sure? He's got to be one of Auerbach's prime targets. Us . . . why should we have him?'

'That's what I asked myself, Prime Minister.' The ultimate cynical truth had dawned slowly. Now he was being given the confirmation. 'Gregory ties up the deal for you but then becomes one hero too many, a man who knows too much and has made too many enemies. Expatriate Britons have no part in the Hunt scheme, and as for Eileen Byrne . . . well, she was just a civil servant.'

There was a long pause, perhaps a full sixty seconds, while the two men stared unblinking at each other. Then: 'Have a good trip back to the States, Mr Lateman.'

'Yes,' said Lateman woodenly.

'I can give you lots of proof that the Americans killed him, you know. After all, they got his brother, didn't they? You know, by the way, that there's no story for you, none whatsoever. You also know that you have precisely twelve hours to get out of Britain.'

Hunt did not take his eyes off the American until he left the room. When he had gone, the Prime Minister stood up and poured himself a whisky from a decanter which stood on a side table. Carrying the drink with him, he slowly left the room.

Sunday night, April 17, and the bar of the Inter-Continental Hotel was as deserted as it had been for many months past. But Zarnuk of the *Washington Post* was there with Roly Smith of *Time* magazine. They were deep in conversation.

Andrei Jameson of the *Chicago Herald Tribune* came in and joined them. 'Double Scotch, heavy on the ice,' he shouted to the barman.

'A lot going on,' Zarnuk was saying. 'I've gotten a good thick story on how it built up.'

Roly Smith nodded his head heavily. 'Looks like there was a major bust over how far the US Administration should get involved. Crisis talks with Auerbach broke down before he even left the airport and it's sure put the Secretary of State's career on the rocks. There's even a story that he's had some sort of nervous breakdown and that Cassover might take over. Have to give it to Hunt though, I didn't think it was in him to pull together this coalition. Where's his strength come from?'

'You noticed that Gregory came and went?' asked Jameson.

Zarnuk responded. 'Something in that? Where'd Gregory go?'

Jameson shrugged: 'Does it matter? He had a part. It was axed, that's all. You saw the results, only a mini riot in Shoe Lane today. Quietest Sunday in London in three years and the same in most major cities up and down the country.'

'Good performance Hunt put on television, didn't he?' It was Roly Smith's turn again. 'National press conference and these two dummies, Commander and Brother, sitting in chairs beside him beaming sweetness and light all over. I couldn't believe it.'

'Right. Here we've been, sitting on our asses for months, sending back copy about this country goin' over and out. Well, you just have to give it to them. The British have it, whatever *it* is. Over the brink, then back on firm ground and they'll be playing cricket again before we know it,' Jameson added morosely.

'Did you hear some story about a big new oil find off the Shetlands?' asked Roly Smith, after a pause.

'A whisper,' said Jameson. 'Hardly top copy at a time like this.'

'Don't know,' said Roly Smith. 'People are beginning to talk about something major.'

The three journalists turned on their stools as a fourth man entered the bar. 'Hi there, Lateman. Where you been hiding all this time?' called Roly.

'Been about. But not much longer,' Lateman said. 'Came in to say that I'm off. See you fellas around somewhere.'

'C'mon, have a drink first,' Zarnuk insisted.

'Just time for one. Then . . . I've got my ticket. New York by tomorrow's Pan Am flight. The party's over here.'

Outside on the pavement again, Dan Lateman, red eyes screwed up tight in his lined white face, stood searching for his car. But it was not his which careered down an almost deserted Park Lane and hooked him off the kerb, dragging his limp and lifeless remains some fifty yards before screaming on into the London night.